A CURSE OF SILVER AND SCARS

A BEAUTY AND THE BEAST RETELLING

LEGENDS REBORN
BOOK FOUR

MARIE-HELENE LEBEAULT

First Edition

Editing by Veronica Jauregui
Cover by Get Covers

CHAPTER I

ARRIVAL

The Blackthorn Estate had been dying for seven years.

Mira Thorne felt it in the discordant hum that set her teeth on edge as she approached the gates—magic gone sour, enchantments warping under the weight of neglect. Most estates simply fell apart when their owners died. This one... held on. And that made it dangerous.

The concealment charms still functioned, keeping the manor hidden from curious travelers on the main road, but barely. She could see the shimmer at the edges where the spells frayed, reality bending like heat waves on a summer day. Whatever was sustaining the magic here had more will than sense.

Mira adjusted her leather satchel, the crystal-threaded tuning rod inside humming faintly against her ribs. The Guild's assignment letter crinkled in her coat pocket as she pushed through the wrought iron gates.

Assess magical decay at Blackthorn Estate. Determine salvageability of existing enchantments. Report findings within fourteen days.

Simple enough, in theory. She'd done dozens of these assessments—though none quite like the disaster in Millhaven, where unstable preservation spells had turned an entire library into carnivorous paper. That had taught her to trust her instincts when magic felt wrong.

And this place felt very wrong indeed.

The path leading up to the house was choked with brambles that grew in unnatural spirals, their thorns gleaming silver despite the autumn air that somehow carried the scent of spring rain. The smell made her pause—weather magic was notoriously difficult to maintain, and seasonal confusion usually meant deep temporal disturbance.

But this was her first assignment to an estate that was still inhabited. The Guild's interest level was unusually high, which meant either valuable magic worth preserving or dangerous magic worth containing. Given the way her skin prickled, she suspected the latter.

The manor squatted ahead like a wounded animal, its gray stone walls streaked with moisture that had no business being there in such dry weather. Ivy crawled up the eastern face in uneven patches, and several upper windows were fogged from the inside, as if the house itself were fogged from the inside, like lungs exhaling mist.

She paused at the front steps, pulling her tuning rod from its case. The crystal threads warmed against her palm, shifting from silver to muddy amber. Emotional residue, thick and bitter as old wine. Whatever lived in this house was deeply, persistently miserable.

The front door was solid oak, carved with protective sigils that looked more like scars now, their lines blurred as if someone had tried to claw them away from the inside.

She raised her hand to knock.

The door swung open before her knuckles made contact.

"Guild assessor, I presume."

The voice was cultured, bored, and edged with practiced disdain. The man standing in the doorway was tall, his dark hair falling across his forehead, hinting at a past vanity that had faded away. His clothes were well-made but wrinkled, and everything about his posture spoke of nobility forced into reduced circumstances.

What caught her attention were the scars.

They traced jagged lines down the left side of his neck and jaw, silver-bright against pale skin like cracked porcelain. Beautiful in an unsettling way, too precise to be accidental. As she watched, they flickered faintly, responding to some internal shift.

"Mira Thorne," she said, extending her hand. "You'd be the caretaker?"

His gray eyes flicked to her outstretched hand—and away again, a moment too slow to be pure disdain. There was something else there, buried beneath the practiced indifference.

"Caretaker, yes. Among other things." He stepped back, gesturing her inside with dismissive courtesy. "I assume you'll want to begin your evaluation immediately."

The way he said 'evaluation' made it sound like an autopsy.

Mira stepped into the foyer, her boots clicking against marble gone gray with age. The air smelled of roses and mildew—beauty rotting from the inside out. Overhead, a crystal chandelier swayed despite the absence of any breeze, and she caught the distant sound of a harpsichord playing a waltz that should have ended decades ago.

The house *noticed* her. She felt it in the shift of air pressure, the way shadows pooled differently when she moved.

"The estate has opinions about visitors," the man said,

3

following her gaze to the swaying fixture. His tone held dark amusement. "I do hope you're not easily rattled, Miss Thorne."

"I'm not easily anything," Mira replied, pulling out her field journal. The enchanted pages hummed as she opened them. "Your name?"

"Does it matter?"

She looked up, meeting his storm-gray gaze. "It matters for my report."

Something flickered across his expression—there and gone too quickly to interpret, but the scars along his jaw pulsed brighter. The walls seemed to lean inward, and her tuning rod grew warm against her ribs.

"Corwin," he said finally. "Though I doubt your Guild will find that particularly illuminating."

No family name. No title, though everything about his bearing screamed aristocracy. She made a note, then clicked her pen against the journal's spine. "I'll need access to all areas of the estate. The Guild's mandate covers structural enchantments, protective wards, climate control, and any specialty work that might require preservation or controlled removal."

"All areas," he repeated, amusement creeping into his voice. The kind that came from watching someone walk toward a cliff. "How thorough of you."

"I'm paid to be thorough. And I've worked in plenty of inadvisable places." She tucked her journal under her arm. "Last month, I cleared a tower where the stairs turned into a slide whenever someone felt 'insufficient reverence' for the owner's work."

Corwin's smile was sharp-edged. "How dreadful. I do hope you weren't injured."

"I wasn't. The client, however, discovered that insufficient reverence includes billing disputes."

The chandelier chimed more insistently overhead, and she could have sworn she heard laughter echoing from the upper floors—too light, too musical to be Corwin's voice.

His expression shifted, becoming calculating. "Very well, Miss Thorne. Let's see how long your professional confidence lasts."

He turned toward the grand staircase, one hand trailing along the banister. The dark wood seemed to respond to his touch, grain shifting like water disturbed by the wind.

"How long have you been caretaker here?" she asked, pulling out her tuning rod. The crystal threads immediately began shifting color—amber to deep gold, shot through with red.

"Time moves strangely in old houses," Corwin replied without turning. "Does it matter if it's been seven years or seventy?"

"For dating the magical decay, yes." She made a note as the rod's colors deepened. "This level of emotional saturation doesn't happen overnight."

He paused at the foot of the staircase. "Seven years, then. Give or take a lifetime."

The tuning rod in her hand was singing now, a low harmonic that spoke of deep magical trauma. "The estate was commissioned by House Blackthorn approximately sixty years ago," she said, reciting from her files. "The family line ended seven years ago."

The quality of silence changed. The house seemed to hold its breath.

"How convenient," Corwin said softly, "that the timeline matches so perfectly."

His voice carried the threadbare weight of someone who'd

worn both grief and bitterness too long to tell the difference. The scars along his jaw pulsed brighter, and when she mentioned the family's end, his free hand moved unconsciously to his throat—fingers pressing against the skin as if feeling for a wound long healed—before he caught himself.

"You knew the family," she said.

"I knew them." His grip tightened on the banister until the wood creaked. "Perhaps better than anyone should have."

Personal connection confirmed. She noted: *Caretaker displays a strong emotional response to family history. Possible—*

A glint of silver caught her eye. High on the wall behind Corwin hung a portrait partially obscured by shadow, but she could make out enough to see dark hair, aristocratic features, and what looked like the same storm-gray eyes. The resemblance was unmistakable, yet the clothing in the painting was clearly from another era.

"That could complicate the assessment," she said carefully, not mentioning the portrait.

Corwin turned to face her fully, and his smile was all sharp edges and dark amusement. "Miss Thorne, I suspect you have no idea how complicated this assessment is about to become."

Every window in the foyer slammed shut.

The sound cracked through the house like thunder, followed by silence so complete it seemed to have weight. The chandelier began swaying violently, crystal pendants striking each other in a discordant symphony. From somewhere above came the sound of footsteps—measured, deliberate—though no one else should be in the house. The rhythm sent an odd chill through her, familiar in a way that made no sense.

Her tuning rod flared white-hot, the crystal burning against her palm. Pain shot up her arm, and her grip tightened to keep from dropping it. This was the kind of reading that preceded catastrophic ward failure.

She didn't flinch, but her pulse jumped. In the sudden darkness, Corwin's scars gleamed like molten silver, and she realized with crystalline clarity that whatever he was, he was no simple caretaker.

"Interesting," he murmured, watching her face. "The house doesn't seem to approve of Guild oversight."

Mira forced her breathing steady despite the magical chaos swirling around them. "The house doesn't get a vote in Guild business."

She met his gaze without flinching, even as the walls pulsed with barely contained energy.

"But you're right about one thing," she continued. "This is definitely going to be complicated."

The house shivered around them, magic rippling through stone and timber like something alive and in pain. Whatever Corwin was—whatever he'd been to the Blackthorn family—the truth was written in silver scars, and the portrait that watched from the shadows, its storm-gray eyes following her as if it, too, had something to say.

CHAPTER 2
HOSTILE MAGIC

The windows stayed shut.

Mira stood in the sudden darkness of the foyer, her tuning rod still singing warnings against her palm, and watched Corwin's face in the silver glow of his scars. He looked almost pleased by the house's tantrum, as if magical rebellion were a mild form of entertainment.

"Well," he said, his voice cutting through the oppressive silence. "Shall we continue the tour? Or would you prefer to file your report from the safety of the doorway?"

The challenge in his tone was unmistakable. Mira tucked her rod away, ignoring the way her hand still ached from its violent reaction. "Lead on. Though you might want to ask your house to behave itself. Structural damage voids most Guild insurance policies."

Something that might have been genuine amusement flickered across his features. "I'll be sure to mention that at our next conversation."

Our next conversation. As if he spoke to the house regularly. She made a mental note as he turned toward the shadowed corridor that branched off from the main hall.

The moment they stepped away from the foyer, the atmosphere changed. The air grew thicker, heavier, pressing against her lungs with each breath. Her boots echoed differently here—not the sharp click of marble, but the muffled sound of wood that had absorbed too much moisture, too much time.

"The east wing," Corwin said, his voice oddly formal. "Where the family's daily life once took place. Breakfast room, morning parlor, the lady's solar." He paused at a doorway, his hand resting on the frame. "Though I suspect you'll find it rather... changed."

Mira pulled out her tuning rod again, letting it hang from its chain. The crystals immediately began to glow, shifting from their normal silver to a sickly yellow-green that made her stomach turn. "When did you last have proper maintenance done on the preservation spells?"

"Maintenance." Corwin's laugh was sharp, bitter. "Miss Thorne, this house hasn't had proper *anything* in seven years."

The rod's glow deepened, and she felt a familiar prickle of warning. Untended preservation magic didn't just fade—it *changed*, becoming something hungry, possessive. She'd seen it before: houses that wouldn't let their occupants leave, rooms that rearranged themselves to trap visitors, walls that whispered secrets that should have been forgotten.

"The magical signatures here are aggressive," she said, making notes as they walked. "Have you experienced any... unusual phenomena?"

Corwin's smile was razor-thin. "You mean beyond the obvious?"

Before she could ask what he meant by obvious, the corridor around them *shifted*.

It was subtle at first—just a sense that the walls had moved closer together, that the ceiling had dropped a few inches. But then the wallpaper began to change, fading from its current deep blue to a lighter shade, then to yellow, then to something that looked like it had been painted with sunshine and children's laughter.

"Fascinating," Corwin murmured, though he sounded more resigned than amazed. "It's showing you what it used to be."

Mira's rod was practically vibrating now, the crystals cycling through colors so rapidly they blurred together. "This level of temporal displacement is dangerous. The house is trying to exist in multiple time periods simultaneously."

"Is that your professional opinion, Miss Thorne?"

She looked at him sharply. There was something in his voice—not quite mockery, but close. As she watched, his scars dimmed slightly, and for just a moment, he looked almost... tired. Defeated.

"It's a fact. Temporal magic requires enormous amounts of energy to maintain. When it starts to fail—"

The walls around them *sobbed*.

The sound was unmistakable—deep, wrenching grief that seemed to come from the very stones. The yellow wallpaper began to streak with what looked like tears, dark stains spreading down toward the floor like old blood.

As the sobbing deepened, a flicker of another time danced at the edges of Mira's vision—sunlight through lace curtains, a woman in blue silk singing softly in what must have been the solar, her voice carrying a lullaby that spoke of love and protection. Then it vanished, as if the house regretted showing too much.

This wasn't just hostile magic—it was heartbroken magic.

Mira's training kicked in. She pulled a piece of silver chalk from her satchel and began sketching stabilization sigils on the nearest wall, her movements quick and precise. "The emotional resonance is feeding back into the temporal displacement," she said, more to herself than to Corwin. "If I can create a buffer—"

"Don't."

The word cracked through the air like a whip. Mira looked up to find Corwin standing rigid, his scars blazing so brightly they cast shadows on the weeping walls. Something about his posture reminded her of a man braced for a blow.

"Don't what?"

"Don't try to fix it." His voice was low, dangerous. "You don't understand what you're dealing with."

"I understand unstable magic when I see it." She turned back to her sigil, adding another line to complete the stabilization matrix. "This level of emotional saturation will—"

The chalk *screamed* when it touched the wall.

The sound was inhuman, agonized—like a bone snapping underwater. It sent shockwaves through the rod in her hand that made her teeth ache and her vision blur. The sigil she'd been drawing began to smoke, then to *bleed*—actual blood seeping from the silver lines as if she'd cut the wall open.

"I warned you," Corwin said quietly, and there was no satisfaction in his voice. Only a weary kind of sorrow.

The corridor around them convulsed. The walls expanded and contracted like lungs struggling for breath, and the weeping wallpaper began to peel away in long strips that moved like living things. The floor beneath their feet tilted at an impossible angle, and for a moment, Mira felt as though she were standing on the side of a ship in a storm.

Her rod went white-hot again, and this time, she couldn't help the sharp intake of breath as the crystal burned against her palm. Her magical channels felt raw, oversaturated as if she'd tried to drink lightning. She forced herself to breathe slowly, to center her energy before the backlash could take hold properly.

"What is this place?" she managed, gripping her rod so tightly that the crystal edges bit into her palm.

"It's angry," Corwin replied, and there was something almost gentle in his voice now. "It doesn't like strangers. And it especially doesn't like being told what to do."

The house settled around them with a sound like a sigh of exhaustion. The walls stopped their breathing motion, the floor leveled itself, and the bleeding sigil faded until only faint silver lines remained. But the feeling of being watched —being *judged*—remained as strong as ever.

Mira stared at the wall where her sigil had been, her hands trembling slightly from the magical overload. "The house is *sentient*."

"Very good, Miss Thorne." His voice held none of its earlier mockery. Now it just sounded... empty. "Top marks for observation."

She turned to face him, and for the first time since they'd met, she saw past his carefully maintained facade of bored aristocracy. There was pain there, deep and old, and something that looked almost like fear.

"How long has it been like this?"

"Seven years," he said simply. "Give or take a lifetime."

The same timeframe again. The same careful non-answer. Mira tucked her chalk away, noting how her hands still shook from the backlash. "Sentient architecture doesn't just *happen*, Corwin. This level of consciousness requires a massive traumatic event, or..." She paused, studying his face. "...a very powerful sacrifice."

Something flickered in his storm-gray eyes—there and gone so quickly she might have imagined it. But she caught the way his hand moved unconsciously to his throat again, fingers pressing against the scarred skin as if it ached.

"Perhaps it does require a sacrifice," he said.

The corridor around them seemed to hold its breath again, waiting.

"Show me one of the changed rooms first," Mira said, gesturing toward the doorway he'd indicated earlier. "I need to understand the scope of the temporal displacement before we go any deeper."

Corwin hesitated for just a moment—long enough for her to notice. Then he pushed open the door to what had once been the morning parlor.

The room beyond was *wrong*.

Not dramatically so, but in a subtle way that made the back of her neck prickle. The furniture rearranged itself as they watched—a settee sliding away from the window, chairs turning to face different directions, a small table walking on delicate legs to position itself beside the fireplace. The movements were slow, deliberate, and almost thoughtful.

"It's trying to accommodate," Corwin said, and there was something almost fond in his voice. "The way it used to when the family had guests."

Above the mantle hung a painting of a young woman in a garden, her face serene and laughing. She wore a gown of deep blue silk, and there was something about the way her dark hair caught the painted sunlight that seemed almost alive. As Mira watched, the woman's features began to age—lines appearing around her eyes, gray threading through her hair, her smile fading into something sadder, more knowing. Then the process reversed, the years falling away until she was young again, caught in eternal spring.

Corwin's gaze lingered on the portrait with an intensity that made Mira's breath catch. There was something in his expression—not just grief, but a kind of desperate hunger, as if he were trying to memorize every brushstroke.

"Who was she?" Mira asked softly.

"Lady Elara Blackthorn," Corwin replied, his voice carefully neutral. But his hand had moved to his throat again, pressing against the scars as if they pained him. "The last of the line."

Mira noticed how the painted woman's eyes were the same storm-gray as Corwin's, how the line of her jaw matched his own aristocratic features. The resemblance was too strong to be coincidental.

"Family resemblance," she murmured, testing.

Corwin's smile was sharp as broken glass. "You could say that."

The fireplace suddenly flared to life with ghostly blue flames that cast no heat. Within the fire, Mira could hear whispers—fragments of conversations, laughter, someone calling a name she couldn't quite make out. The voices layered over each other like echoes from different decades, a palimpsest of sound.

"The house remembers," she said, pulling out her journal to record what she was seeing. "It's trying to recreate the past."

"It remembers everything," Corwin agreed. "Every word spoken in these rooms, every tear shed, every..." He stopped abruptly, his jaw clenching.

Every what? Mira wanted to ask, but something in his expression warned her off. Instead, she approached the fireplace, letting her tuning rod hang free. The crystals immediately began cycling through colors—silver to gold to deep crimson to black, then back again in endless repetition.

She pulled out a small recording crystal, standard equipment for any Guild assessment. The moment she activated it, the crystal began to smoke, its surface clouding over as if exposed to acid.

"The temporal displacement is interfering with standard documentation," she muttered, tucking the ruined crystal away. "Whatever happened here, it's created a dead zone for most magical instruments."

In the flames, one of the dancing figures suddenly turned toward her. For just a moment, their eyes met across the barrier between memory and present, and Mira felt a chill that had nothing to do with the ghostly fire. The figure's mouth moved as if trying to speak, but no sound emerged beyond the whispered chorus.

"The magical resonance here is incredible," she said, making notes by hand. "I've never seen emotional saturation this deep. It would take years of intense feeling to create this kind of imprint."

"Yes," Corwin said quietly. "It would."

She looked up at him, studying the way the blue flames reflected in his eyes. "You were here when it happened. When the house became... this."

It wasn't a question, and he didn't deny it.

"I was here," he confirmed. "I was here for all of it."

The flames in the fireplace suddenly roared higher, and for just a moment, Mira thought she saw shapes dancing in them—figures in formal dress, spinning through a waltz that existed only in memory. One couple at the center of the dance looked familiar: a woman in blue silk, her face radiant with joy, and a man whose profile matched Corwin's exactly.

Then the fire died back to its ghostly flicker, and the whispers faded to silence.

"Show me the rest," Mira said finally, tucking her journal away. "All of it."

Running would be safer. Smarter. But she'd seen what

happened when assessors turned away too soon—how rot spread, how families vanished into magical catastrophes that could have been prevented. She'd sworn never to be one of them, no matter the personal cost.

Corwin's smile returned, but it was different now—sharper, more dangerous, with an edge of something that might have been desperation. "Are you certain, Miss Thorne? The house has only just begun to introduce itself."

As if summoned by his words, a door at the far end of the corridor swung open with a creak that sounded almost like laughter. Beyond it lay darkness so complete it seemed solid, and from that darkness came the faint sound of music—not the harpsichord from before, but something deeper, sadder. A funeral dirge played on strings that wept with every note.

The melody tugged at something in Mira's chest, a sense of loss so profound it made her breath catch. It spoke of endings, of things precious and irretrievable, of love that had turned to ash. For a moment she felt tears prick at her eyes, though she couldn't say why.

"After you," Corwin said, gesturing toward the open door with mock courtesy. But his scars were pulsing in rhythm with the distant music, and she caught the way his breathing had gone shallow.

Mira looked at the waiting darkness, then at the man beside her with his glowing scars and too-knowing eyes. Every instinct she'd developed over years of magical assessment was screaming at her to retreat, to file a report recommending immediate demolition, to get as far away from this place as possible.

Instead, she stepped forward into the dark.

Behind her, she heard Corwin's soft laughter, and the sound followed her like a promise. Or a threat.

The door swung shut behind them with a sound like a

finality, and Mira realized that whatever game she'd walked into, the house—and Corwin—had just changed the rules.

Her tuning rod pulsed once against her ribs, a final warning before its glow faded entirely.

In the darkness ahead, something was waiting. And from the way Corwin's breathing had changed, from the way his scars had begun to pulse in time with that mournful dirge, she suspected he knew exactly what it was.

The hostile magic of this place wasn't just dangerous—it was deeply, personally wounded. And she was about to discover why.

CHAPTER 3
THE HEART OF MEMORY

The darkness beyond the door wasn't empty.

It breathed with the rhythm of old grief, thick and suffocating, pressing against Mira's skin like velvet drapes heavy with moisture. The funeral dirge grew stronger as they moved forward, though she couldn't tell if they were walking down a corridor or floating through space —her boots made no sound, and the walls seemed to exist only as suggestions at the edges of her vision.

"The music room," Corwin said, his voice oddly distant. "Lady Elara spent her evenings here."

Mira pulled out her tuning rod, but the crystals remained stubbornly dark. Whatever force governed this space had rules different from the rest of the house. "I can't get readings here."

"No," Corwin agreed. "This room doesn't care much for measurement."

The darkness began to thin, revealing glimpses of familiar shapes—a pianoforte, sheets of music scattered across a Persian carpet, tall windows draped in midnight blue. But everything was wrong as if viewed through water or tears.

The furniture aged and restored itself in slow cycles, elegant curves becoming worn and shabby before polishing themselves back to perfection.

Then the light stabilized, and Mira's breath caught.

The room was beautiful. Hauntingly, impossibly beautiful, like a jewel preserved in amber. Moonlight streamed through the windows with the quality of captured dreams, illuminating a woman seated at the pianoforte.

Lady Elara Blackthorn.

She was younger than in the portrait downstairs, her dark hair unbound and spilling over her shoulders like ink. Her fingers moved across the keys with heartbreaking precision, drawing music from the instrument that seemed to come from her very soul. The same storm-gray eyes that had watched from the portrait were fixed on something beyond the music, beyond the room—on a future that Mira somehow knew would never come.

"She's beautiful," Mira whispered.

Beside her, Corwin made a sound that might have been pain. "She was."

The woman at the piano turned then, and her gaze found Corwin across the span of years with the accuracy of a lodestone finding true north. Her face transformed—grief replaced by radiant joy, love so pure it made the air itself seem to glow.

"My heart," she said, her voice carrying despite the distance, despite the impossibility of it all. "You've come back to me."

Corwin's scars flared brilliant silver, and Mira felt the temperature in the room plummet. "Elara." The name was torn from his throat like a confession.

The scene before them flickered—reality asserting itself in fragments. For a moment, Mira saw the room as it truly was:

dust-covered furniture draped in sheets, the pianoforte's keys yellowed with age, windows fogged with years of neglect. Then the memory reasserted itself, and Elara was there again, rising from the bench with inhuman grace.

"You look tired," Elara said, moving toward them with steps that left no footprints on the carpet. "Are you not sleeping?"

Corwin's breathing had gone ragged, and when Mira glanced at him, she saw his hands clenched into fists at his sides. "I sleep," he said roughly.

Elara's smile was gentle, knowing. "Liar. You never could lie to me properly." She reached toward him, her fingers stopping just short of his cheek. "You're fading, my love. This existence... it's killing you."

"I deserve to fade." The words were barely audible, but they struck the room like a physical blow. The windows rattled in their frames, and the music from the piano shifted to a minor key that spoke of desolation.

"No." Elara's voice carried absolute authority, the kind of love that brooked no argument. "Don't say that. What happened—"

"Was my fault." Corwin's scars were pulsing now, their light casting harsh shadows across his face. "I failed you. I failed everyone."

Mira found herself stepping backward, instinctively recognizing that she was witnessing something too intimate, too raw for an outsider's eyes. But the darkness behind her had solidified into a wall—the room wouldn't let her leave.

The memory around them began to fracture, reality bleeding through in jagged cuts. One moment, Elara stood before them in moonlight and shadow; the next, the room was empty, filled only with the accusatory silence of abandonment. The pianoforte played itself, keys depressing without touch, drawing out melodies that sounded like accusations.

"She loved music," Corwin said suddenly, his voice hollow. "Especially at night, when the rest of the house was sleeping. She said it was when her soul felt most free."

The temperature dropped further, and Mira's breath began to mist. "Corwin, we need to leave. This level of temporal displacement—"

"Will what?" He turned toward her, and his eyes held the wild intensity of a man balancing on a knife's edge. "Drive me mad? Make me forget the difference between past and present?" His laugh was sharp enough to cut. "Too late for that, Miss Thorne."

As if responding to his words, the room around them shattered.

The walls dissolved into fragments of memory—dozens of scenes playing simultaneously like a kaleidoscope of the past. Mira saw Elara dancing alone in the moonlight, her gown trailing behind her like liquid shadow. She saw her bent over books in what must have been the library, reading aloud in a voice like music. She saw her gardening with dirt-stained hands and laughing with pure joy, saw her weeping over a letter whose contents remained hidden, saw her standing at the window watching for someone who never came.

And in every scene, Corwin was there—sometimes visible, sometimes just a shadow at the edge of perception, watching with the desperate hunger of a man starving for something he could never have again.

"The house is trying to drive me away," Mira realized, her voice steadier than she felt. "It doesn't want me to see this."

"The house," Corwin said softly, "is protecting us both."

The fragments of memory suddenly cohered into a single scene, more vivid than anything they'd witnessed before.

Elara stood in this same room, but her face was different—older, marked by lines of sorrow that hadn't been there in the earlier visions. She wore a gown of midnight blue, and her hands were pressed to her heart as if it pained her.

"I can't wait any longer," she was saying to someone beyond the frame of the memory. "The curse is consuming everything. If I don't act now—"

The scene cut off abruptly, leaving only the echo of her words and the scent of roses touched by frost.

Corwin had gone rigid beside her. "No," he whispered. "Not this. She doesn't need to see this."

But the memory was already reforming, and this time, Mira saw what the house had been trying to hide. Elara stood at the center of a ritual circle drawn in what looked suspiciously like silver and salt, her hands glowing with power that seemed to come from her very life force. The air around her shimmered with the kind of magic that required enormous sacrifice—the kind that carved permanent scars on the soul.

Mira had studied magical sacrifice in dusty Guild textbooks, but nothing had prepared her for the aching beauty of someone choosing to become memory itself.

"The preservation spells," she breathed, understanding flooding through her. "She created them herself."

"She was trying to save the estate," Corwin said, his voice barely audible. "The family magic was failing, had been failing for generations. The house was dying, and with it, everything the Blackthorns had built. So she..." He stopped, his throat working as if the words were too large to swallow.

"She bound her life force to the estate's magic," Mira finished. The pieces were falling into place with horrible clarity. "That's why the house is sentient. That's why it responds to emotion. She's still here."

The memory showed Elara speaking words in the old

tongue, her voice growing weaker with each syllable as the power flowed out of her and into the stones, the timbers, and the very air of the house. Her life, her soul, her essence—all of it poured into the preservation of a place and its memories.

This wasn't just memory—it was the heart of it, still beating beneath layers of magic and grief.

"She was dying anyway," Corwin said, and his voice held the hollow quality of someone who'd rehearsed these words a thousand times. "The curse that took the family line—it was in her blood, eating her from the inside. She had perhaps a year left, maybe less."

Mira felt her throat tighten. "So, she chose to die on her own terms."

"She chose to die for something." His scars were blazing now, their light almost too bright to look at directly. "To save what could be saved."

The ritual reached its crescendo in the memory before them. Elara's form grew transparent as her life force flowed into the waiting spell matrix, her face serene despite the magnitude of what she was sacrificing. But just before the magic claimed her entirely, she turned toward something—someone—outside the circle.

"Promise me," she said, her voice growing faint as starlight. "Promise me you'll find a way to be happy."

And Corwin's voice, younger and desperate: "I promise. But only if you promise to wait for me."

Her smile was radiant even as she faded. "Always, my heart. Always."

The memory shattered like glass, leaving them standing in the dusty reality of the abandoned music room. But the echo of that promise lingered in the air, heavy as incense, binding as chains.

Mira turned to look at Corwin, really look at him, and saw

the truth written in every line of his face. The scars weren't just marks—they were magical scarring, the kind that came from binding one's life force to something larger than oneself. He'd found a way to tie his existence to hers, to the house, to the magic that kept her consciousness alive in stone and timber.

"You're not the caretaker," she said quietly. "You're part of the preservation spell."

His smile was as bitter as the winter wind. "Very good, Miss Thorne. Though 'part of' rather understates the situation."

The room around them began to fade, the walls becoming translucent as the house prepared to reveal its next secret. But Mira had seen enough for now. She understood the scope of what she was dealing with, the impossible tangle of love and loss and magic that had created this place.

"How long have you been bound here?" she asked.

"Seven years," Corwin replied. "Give or take a lifetime."

For the first time since they'd met, his answer was entirely literal.

The house shivered around them, and somewhere in the distance, a door opened with a soft sigh of inevitability. There was more to see, more to understand, but Mira's hands were shaking from magical overload, and the weight of what she'd witnessed pressed against her chest like a physical entity.

She looked at Corwin—at this man who'd bound himself to years of haunted existence for the love of someone he could never truly touch again—and felt something shift in her chest. Pity, perhaps. Or recognition.

"The Guild will want to know if the magic can be safely removed," she said carefully.

Corwin's laugh was soft, broken. "And what will you tell them, Miss Thorne?"

Mira looked around the music room, at the dust motes dancing in the afternoon sunlight that somehow felt like moonbeams, at the pianoforte that still hummed with the echo of love songs. She thought of Elara's sacrifice, of Corwin's years of faithful vigil, of a house that remembered every moment of joy and sorrow it had ever contained.

"I don't know yet," she said honestly. "But I'm beginning to understand that this isn't just about magical preservation."

"No," Corwin agreed. "It's about keeping faith with the dead."

As they left the music room, Mira caught a glimpse of movement in her peripheral vision—a woman in blue silk, watching them go with eyes full of ancient sadness and impossible hope.

CHAPTER 4
THE WEIGHT OF TRUTH

T he afternoon sun slanted through the tall windows of what had once been the Blackthorn library, casting geometric patterns across shelves that held more dust than books. Mira sat cross-legged on the Persian carpet, her field journal spread before her like a battle plan, though the words she'd written made little sense in the harsh light of day.

Sentient architecture. Temporal displacement. Life force preservation matrix. Recommend... what?

She pressed the heels of her hands against her eyes, trying to ease the pressure building behind them. Her tuning rod lay silent in its case—after the music room, it had refused to function properly, the crystals remaining stubbornly dark no matter which magical signatures she tried to read.

"Professional difficulties, Miss Thorne?"

Corwin's voice came from the doorway, carrying its usual thread of dark amusement. When she looked up, he stood silhouetted against the hallway's gloom, a tea service balanced on a silver tray that gleamed despite seven years of neglect.

"The house cleaned it," he said, following her gaze to the spotless silver. "It has opinions about hospitality."

Mira closed her journal, grateful for the interruption. "Does it have opinions about everything?"

"Oh, yes." Corwin set the tray on a low table that definitely hadn't been there moments before. "It's quite opinionated, actually. Judgmental, some might say."

The tea was perfect—exactly the right temperature, steeped to the precise shade of amber she preferred. Mira didn't ask how the house could know such things. After the music room, she was learning to accept impossibilities as simple facts.

The tea reminded her, painfully, of another cup shared years ago with someone who had paid attention to such details. Thomas Whitmore. The name still carried the ghost of possibility, of a future she'd chosen not to pursue. He'd been a fellow Guild scholar, brilliant and kind, with a laugh that could fill empty rooms. But when he'd asked her to consider a research partnership that might have become something more, she'd chosen career advancement over personal risk. "Professional relationships compromise objectivity," she'd told herself. "Better to maintain appropriate boundaries." Now, watching a house that loved so completely it had learned to think, she wondered what boundaries had really protected her from—and what they'd cost her.

"You've been writing for three hours," Corwin observed, settling into the chair across from her with fluid grace. "I'm curious what conclusions you've reached."

Mira took a sip of tea, buying time. Everything she'd built —her reputation, her authority—rested on adherence to magical law. But what use was law if it couldn't make space for something like this? The truth was, she had no idea what to write in her report. How did one explain to the Guild that a house was kept alive by love? That the magic they'd been sent to evaluate was actually a woman's soul, spread through stone and timber like roots intertwining through earth and rock.

"The preservation spells are unlike anything in Guild records," she said carefully. "The binding mechanisms alone..."

"Are illegal under current magical statutes," Corwin finished. "Yes, I imagine they would be."

His tone was matter-of-fact, but she caught the tension in his shoulders, the way his fingers drummed against his teacup's rim. He was waiting for judgment—from her, from the Guild, from a world that had very specific ideas about what magic should and shouldn't do.

"Life force binding has been prohibited for over a century," Mira said. "The Guild classifies it as dark magic."

"And yet here we are." Corwin's smile held no warmth. "A testament to the power of love over law."

Something in his voice made her look at him more carefully. In the afternoon light, she could see details that had been hidden in shadow—the way his clothes, though well-made, hung slightly loose, as if he'd lost weight recently. The faint tremor in his hands that he tried to hide. The pallor that spoke of too little sleep, too little sustenance.

"When did you last leave the estate?" she asked.

The question seemed to catch him off-guard. "Leave? Why would I leave?"

"For supplies. Food. Contact with the outside world." She gestured toward the tea service. "This can't all be magical conjuration."

Corwin's laugh was sharp. "Can't it? You've seen what this place is capable of, Miss Thorne. Why assume it follows normal rules about anything?"

But there was something evasive in his manner, a careful

deflection that made her suspect he was hiding something. She thought of the way the house had reacted to her presence, the almost desperate quality of its attempts to recreate the past.

"The binding spell," she said slowly. "It's not just connecting you to the house. It's... consuming you."

Corwin went very still. "That's a rather dramatic conclusion."

"Is it wrong?"

For a long moment, he said nothing. Then he set down his teacup with deliberate precision, the porcelain clicking against the saucer like a small bone breaking.

"The magic requires an anchor," he said finally. "Something to tether Elara's essence to the physical world. I provide that anchor."

"At what cost?"

His scars pulsed brighter, responding to some internal shift. "Everything has a cost, Miss Thorne. The question is whether the price is worth paying."

Mira felt a chill that had nothing to do with the temperature. "How long do you have?"

"Difficult to say. Time moves strangely here, as you've observed." He rose from his chair with careful movements, crossing to the window that overlooked what had once been Elara's garden. "Perhaps a year. Perhaps less."

The casual way he said it made her breath catch. "There has to be another way. Some method of stabilizing the magic without—"

"Without sacrificing myself?" Corwin turned back toward her, and his expression was almost gentle. "I appreciate the concern, truly. But I chose this binding freely, with full knowledge of its consequences."

"Seven years ago, when you were grieving and desperate."

The words came out sharper than she'd intended. "That's hardly informed consent."

Something dangerous flickered in his eyes. "Careful, Miss Thorne. You're beginning to sound as though you care about my welfare."

The warning was clear, but Mira pressed forward anyway. "Why shouldn't I? You're dying to preserve something that's already gone. Elara is dead, Corwin. What you're keeping alive here... it's just an echo."

The temperature in the room plummeted. Frost began forming on the windows, and the books on the shelves rustled as if stirred by an angry wind. Corwin's scars blazed so brightly they cast shadows, and when he spoke, his voice carried the weight of barely controlled fury.

"*Just* an echo?" he repeated softly. "Is that your professional assessment?"

The walls around them began to groan, wood and stone protesting under some invisible pressure. Mira's abandoned teacup rattled against its saucer, and dust rained down from the ceiling as the house itself seemed agreeing with Corwin's anger.

"I didn't mean—" she began.

"You meant exactly what you said." Corwin took a step toward her, and she could see the wild desperation lurking beneath his composure. "She's an echo. A memory. A ghost haunting a dead building. Is that it?"

The air between them shimmered, and suddenly Elara was there—translucent but unmistakably present, her midnight blue gown rustling as she moved between them. Her storm-gray eyes were sad but resolute as she looked from Corwin to Mira and back again.

"Enough," Elara said, her voice carrying the authority of someone accustomed to being obeyed. "Both of you, enough."

Corwin's anger crumbled at the sight of her. "Elara, I—"

"You're frightening our guest." Elara's tone was gentle but firm. "And Miss Thorne, you're hurting someone I love. Neither is acceptable in my house."

Mira found herself stammering an apology to a woman who'd been dead for years, which should have been absurd but somehow felt perfectly natural. "I'm sorry. I spoke without thinking."

"You spoke with passion," Elara corrected, moving closer. Up close, Mira could see that she wasn't entirely solid—sunlight passed through her like she was made of colored glass. "There's no shame in that. But passion without understanding can be cruel."

She turned toward Corwin, and her expression softened into something so tender it made Mira's chest ache. "Show her," Elara said quietly. "Show her what this really is."

Corwin shook his head violently. "She's Guild, Elara. She'll report everything she sees."

"She knew someone would come eventually," Corwin murmured, his voice thick with emotion. "She hoped it would be someone who listened."

"Will you?" Elara asked, fixing Mira with those impossible gray eyes. "Report everything you see here?"

Mira looked between them—the woman who had chosen to become magic itself, and the man who had bound his life to hers across the barrier of death. She thought of Guild protocols, of magical statutes, of reports that reduced love to clinical terminology.

"I don't know," she said honestly. "I don't know what to report anymore."

Elara smiled, and for a moment, the whole room seemed to glow with warm light. "Then perhaps it's time you understood what you're truly evaluating."

She reached toward Corwin, her translucent fingers not quite touching his cheek. "Take her to the observatory, my heart. Show her the stars."

Before Corwin could protest, Elara turned back to Mira. "The magic here isn't just preservation, Miss Thorne. It's transformation. Evolution. We've become something new— something the Guild has no words for yet."

The air shimmered, and she was gone, leaving only the faint scent of roses and the echo of impossible promises.

Corwin stood frozen where she'd left him, his hand raised as if to touch the space where she'd been. His scars had dimmed to a faint silver glow, and in the afternoon light streaming through the windows, he looked exhausted, fragile.

"The observatory," Mira said quietly.

He nodded without looking at her. "At the top of the north tower. Elara's favorite room in the house." His voice was thick with emotion barely held in check. "She studied astronomy. Said the stars reminded her that even the darkest nights eventually ended."

As they left the library, Mira caught sight of her reflection in one of the tall mirrors that lined the hallway. She looked different somehow—less certain, more conflicted. The Guild assessor who had arrived that morning would have filed a straightforward report recommending immediate magical containment.

But that woman hadn't watched love transcend death, hadn't seen sacrifice transform into something beautiful and terrible and entirely beyond regulation.

The north tower stairs were narrow and steep, winding upward through stone that hummed with old magic. With each step, Mira felt the weight of the house's attention settling over her like a mantle. It was evaluating her just as thoroughly as she was evaluating it, and she had the unsettling feeling that her assessment mattered far more than any report she might file.

At the top of the stairs, Corwin paused before a heavy oak door carved with astronomical symbols. His hand hovered over the latch as if he were gathering courage.

"Fair warning," he said without turning around. "What you're about to see... it will change how you understand everything."

Mira thought of Elara's words—*transformation, evolution, something new*—and felt her pulse quicken. "Then open the door."

He did.

The observatory beyond was like stepping into the night sky itself. The domed ceiling was made entirely of crystal, flawless and clear, showing the afternoon sky in perfect detail. But that wasn't what made Mira's breath catch.

The room was full of light—not sunlight, but something deeper, more alive. It flowed like water through the air, pooling in corners and streaming between furniture that existed in multiple time periods simultaneously. Mira saw the room as it had been in Elara's time—cluttered with star charts and gleaming instruments—and as it was now, empty but somehow more beautiful for its emptiness.

And everywhere, woven through the light like silver thread through fabric, was the presence of something vast and patient and infinitely loving.

The truth weighed on her like gravity—the kind that didn't pull downward but inward, anchoring her to something vast and unknowable.

"This is where it began," Corwin said softly. "Where Elara first mapped the stars that would guide her final spell. And this..." He gestured toward the flowing light, the impossible beauty that surrounded them. "This is what she became."

Mira stepped further into the room, her hands outstretched as if she could touch the streaming radiance. Where it brushed her skin, she felt a warmth that spoke of summer evenings and laughter shared in darkness, of love that refused to be bounded by something as small as death.

"She's not just preserved here," she whispered, understanding flooding through her. "She's grown. Changed. Become something more than human."

"And so have I," Corwin said. "The binding doesn't just anchor her essence—it's transforming me as well. Day by day, year by year, until..." He stopped, his throat working.

"Until you become like her," Mira finished. "Part of the magic itself."

He nodded, and there was something almost like relief in his expression. "The Guild would call it an abomination. But Miss Thorne... it's the most beautiful thing I've ever experienced. To feel her presence always, to know that love can truly transcend anything... how do I choose my old mortality over this?"

The light in the room pulsed brighter, responding to his words, and Mira felt tears pricking at her eyes. This wasn't the dark magic described in Guild textbooks. This was something entirely new—love made manifest, binding two souls across the boundary between life and death.

But it was also consumption, transformation, and the slow dissolution of individual identity into something larger. And watching Corwin's face as he spoke of it, she saw both ecstasy and terror warring in his expression.

"What happens if the Guild intervenes?" she asked.

Corwin's scars pulsed once, sharply. "The binding breaks. Elara's essence disperses. I die." His smile was bitter. "And all of this—every moment of beauty, every memory preserved— becomes nothing more than an empty house full of dust."

The weight of responsibility settled on Mira's shoulders like a stone. Whatever she wrote in her report would determine not just the fate of the estate, but the survival of something unprecedented in magical history.

She looked around the observatory, at the impossible light that spoke of transcendent love, and realized that some things were more important than Guild protocols.

The question was: what was she willing to risk to protect them?

CHAPTER 5
LINES DRAWN IN SILVER

The message crystal arrived at dawn, its harsh red glow cutting through the soft luminescence that filled Mira's guest room. She'd barely slept, her mind churning with images of flowing light and Corwin's desperate confession, but the crystal's insistent chiming drove away any hope of rest.

She touched the faceted surface, and Guild Master Aldric's voice filled the room with clipped authority.

"Thorne. Your preliminary report was due yesterday. The Council grows impatient with this assessment. Submit your findings within twelve hours, or we'll send Enforcer Tavian to conclude the evaluation. The Blackthorn situation has drawn attention from the capital."

The crystal went dark, leaving Mira staring at her reflection in its silent surface. Enforcer Tavian—she knew that name. He was the Guild's solution to problems that couldn't be reasoned with, a man who approached magical anomalies with the subtlety of a scythe through wheat.

If Tavian came here, there would be no gentle evaluation, no careful consideration of unprecedented circumstances. He would see dark magic and respond accordingly, reducing seven years of love and sacrifice to ash and regulation.

A soft knock at her door interrupted her spiraling thoughts. "Miss Thorne?" Corwin's voice carried none of its usual mockery. "Might I have a word?"

She opened the door to find him standing in the hallway, still dressed in yesterday's clothes. His scars were dim in the morning light, but she could see the tension in every line of his frame.

"You heard," she said. It wasn't a question.

"The house has excellent acoustics." His smile was brittle. "Guild business, I take it?"

Mira stepped aside, letting him enter. The guest room was small but comfortable, furnished with pieces that seemed to shift subtly between time periods—a writing desk that aged and restored itself, curtains that changed from summer silk to winter velvet with her breathing.

"They want my report," she said, closing the door behind him. "Today."

Corwin moved to the window, gazing out at the garden where morning mist clung to overgrown hedges. "And what will you tell them?"

The question hung between them. Mira looked at her journal, at the pages of notes that reduced miracle to measurement, love to liability.

"The truth," she said finally.

"Which truth?" Corwin turned toward her, and she saw something fragile in his expression. "That we're an abomination that violates magical law? Or that we're something unprecedented that might change how the Guild understands life and death?"

Before she could answer, the air in the room shimmered, and Elara materialized beside the writing desk. She was more solid than Mira had seen her before, her presence carrying weight and substance that made the furniture around her seem less real.

"The Guild won't care about precedent," Elara said, her voice carrying the authority of someone who had once navigated court politics. "They'll see only threat and violation. They always do."

Mira felt a chill that had nothing to do with magical cold. "You know what they'll do."

"I know what they've done before." Elara's expression darkened. "The Whitmore Estate in '67. The Ashford Manor incident. When the Guild encounters magic it cannot control, it destroys rather than attempts understanding."

Corwin's scars flared brighter. "Elara—"

"No." Her voice cut through his protest like a blade. "Miss Thorne deserves to know what her report will unleash. Tell her about the Whitmore children, my heart. Tell her how the Guild preserved public safety."

The temperature in the room plummeted, and Mira saw Corwin's face go pale. Whatever the Whitmore incident had been, it clearly haunted him.

"The Whitmore Estate was... different," he said carefully. "A family attempting to achieve immortality through blood magic. When the Guild intervened—"

"They killed everyone," Elara finished, her translucent form blazing with cold fire. "Three generations, from grandparents to infants. They called it containment."

Mira felt her stomach turn. "The children couldn't have been complicit—"

"The children were carriers," Corwin said, his voice hollow. "The blood magic had infected their very essence. The Guild determined that killing them was the only way to prevent spread."

"And were they right?" Mira asked, though she dreaded the answer.

The silence stretched like a held breath. Finally, Elara spoke, her voice soft with old grief.

"We'll never know. The Guild doesn't leave room for alternatives."

Mira sank into the chair by her writing desk, the weight of responsibility crushing down on her shoulders. "What you're asking me to do... lying to the Guild, falsifying a report... it's treason against everything I've sworn to uphold."

"We're not asking you to lie," Corwin said gently. "We're asking you to choose which truth matters more."

The morning light streaming through the window caught the edges of Elara's form, turning her into something made of captured starlight. She moved closer to Mira, her presence bringing warmth that had nothing to do with temperature.

"You've seen what we are," Elara said. "Not the magic itself, but what it's created. What it's preserving. Is that worth protecting?"

Mira thought of the observatory, of light that flowed like love made visible, of music that played memories across the boundary between life and death. She thought of Corwin's devotion, years of faithful vigil, and Elara's sacrifice that had transformed death into something beautiful and strange.

But she also thought of Guild law, of magical statutes written in blood and necessity, of the careful balance that kept dangerous magic from consuming the world.

"I need to understand something," she said, looking between them. "The curse that killed your family line—what exactly was it?"

Elara and Corwin exchanged a glance heavy with unspoken communication. Finally, Elara spoke, her voice careful.

"The Blackthorn family was bound to this land through generations of blood magic. Our ancestors made pacts with forces they didn't fully understand, trading pieces of their humanity for power and longevity."

"Each generation paid a price," Corwin continued. "Shortened lifespans, madness, children born with magic that consumed them from within. Elara was the culmination—the last inheritor of a bloodline that had spent itself pursuing immortality."

Mira felt pieces clicking into place. "So when she bound her life force to the estate..."

"I broke the pattern," Elara said simply. "Instead of the magic consuming me, I chose to become it. To transform rather than be destroyed."

"And you followed her," Mira said to Corwin.

His scars pulsed once, bright as stars. "I couldn't let her face eternity alone."

The simple honesty of it hit Mira like a physical blow. A new sound interrupted her thoughts—the distant rumble of carriage wheels on gravel. All three of them froze, listening as the sound grew closer, accompanied by the measured clip of multiple horses.

"Guild transport," Mira breathed.

Corwin moved to the window, his face going ashen. "Four riders. Military formation." He turned toward Mira, his expression grim. "The Council grows impatient with this assessment. Submit your findings within twenty-four hours, or we'll send Enforcer Tavian to conclude the evaluation.."

The house itself seemed to react to the approaching threat. The walls groaned with tension, and Mira felt the air pressure shift as defensive enchantments began to activate. Her abandoned teacup rattled against its saucer, and the curtains stirred despite the absence of any breeze.

"How long do we have?" Elara asked, her form flickering with agitation.

"Minutes," Mira replied, her mind racing. She looked at her journal, at the report she'd been struggling to write, and made a decision that would change everything.

She grabbed her pen and began writing rapidly, her hand moving across the page with desperate speed. She'd drawn her line in silver ink and honest defiance—and there would be no stepping back from it.

Blackthorn Estate assessment complete. Magical signatures consistent with standard preservation enchantments. No evidence of illegal life-force binding detected. Recommend routine maintenance and continued Guild monitoring. Signed, Assessor Mira Thorne.

The words stared back at her from the page, each letter a small act of treason. Her hand trembled as she reached for the sealing wax, and suddenly, the weight of what she'd done crashed over her like a tide.

This wasn't just bending regulations or overlooking minor infractions. This was outright falsification of a Guild assessment—a crime that carried penalties ranging from career destruction to magical binding to prevent future violations. She was throwing away everything she'd built, everything she'd sworn to uphold, for people she'd known for less than a week.

Her fingers hovered over the report, and for a moment, she could almost see herself crossing out the lies, writing the truth: *Unprecedented consciousness preservation achieved through illegal life-force binding. Subjects display complete magical integration. Recommend immediate Guild intervention and controlled study.*

It would be the safe choice. The professional choice. The choice that would preserve her career, her reputation, her carefully constructed life of measured distances and regulated magic.

But as the thought formed, she heard Elara's voice echoing in her memory: "Promise you'll find a way to love me in whatever form I become." Seven years of devotion, of choosing transformation over preservation, of refusing to let death end a love story that had learned to rewrite the very laws of existence.

When had she last felt that kind of certainty? When had she last encountered something worth protecting regardless of personal cost?

The sound of approaching hoofbeats grew louder—Tavian and his escort drew closer with each passing moment. Decision time was running out, and hesitation would damn them all.

Mira looked around the guest room one final time, seeing it with new eyes. The writing desk that had arranged itself perfectly for her needs. The curtains that shifted between seasons according to her mood. The teacup that had appeared each morning filled with exactly the blend she preferred, prepared by a house that had learned to love by watching its inhabitants love each other.

This wasn't just about protecting Corwin and Elara. This was about defending the possibility that magic could be more than regulation and measurement, that love could transcend every boundary the Guild had established, that some things in the world were too precious to be reduced to clinical terminology.

Her hand steadied as she reached for the sealing wax again. The hot red drops fell onto the parchment like small sacrifices, binding her to a choice that would change everything.

"There," she said, holding up the false document. *"Your protection, bought with my career."*

The admission hung in the air between them, weighted with finality. She had crossed a line she could never uncross, chosen loyalty over law in a way that would define everything that followed.

Corwin stared at her in amazement. "You'd risk everything for strangers?"

"You're not strangers anymore," Mira said simply, though the words felt like stepping off a cliff into unknown territory. "And what you've built here... it's worth preserving."

But even as she spoke, she felt the ghost-weight of the truthful report she'd almost written, the safe choice that would have preserved her old life at the cost of something irreplaceable. The woman who had arrived at Blackthorn Estate five days ago would never have made this choice.

That woman was gone now, replaced by someone who had seen love transcend death and chosen to protect it rather than dissect it.

The sound of boots on gravel grew louder, accompanied by harsh voices and the jingle of military equipment. Through the window, Mira could see figures in Guild black approaching the front entrance, their movements efficient and threatening.

Elara moved toward the door, her form solidifying with purpose. "I'll greet our guests. Tavian has always been... direct in his methods."

"Elara, no," Corwin said urgently. "If he sees you—"

"He'll see what I choose to show him," she replied, her voice carrying the steel of aristocratic authority. "A fading echo, perhaps. The last whisper of a dying house. Nothing more."

She turned toward Mira, and for a moment, her eyes

blazed with something that transcended human emotion. "Thank you," she said softly. "For seeing us as we truly are."

Then she was gone, leaving only the faint scent of roses and the echo of gratitude.

Mira tucked the false report into her satchel, her hands trembling with the magnitude of what she'd done. Outside, she could hear Enforcer Tavian's voice, cold and clipped, as he questioned someone—probably a servant conjured by the house's magic.

"What happens now?" Corwin asked.

Mira shouldered her satchel, straightening her Guild robes with hands that barely shook. "Now I go downstairs and convince a Guild Enforcer that there's nothing here worth investigating."

Corwin's scars pulsed brighter, and for a moment, she saw past his careful composure to the gratitude and fear warring beneath. "And after that?"

"After that..." Mira paused at the door, considering. "After that, you and Elara continue becoming whatever it is you're becoming. And I learn to live with having chosen love over law."

Mira descended the stairs to meet Enforcer Tavian carrying secrets that could destroy her career and a lie that might save something unprecedented in magical history.

And for the first time since arriving at Blackthorn Estate, Mira Thorne knew exactly who she was choosing to be.

ENFORCER TAVIAN STOOD in the foyer like a blade waiting to be drawn. He was younger than Mira had expected, with pale eyes that missed nothing and an economy of movement that spoke of violence held in careful check. His Guild uniform was immaculate, his bearing military-precise, and when he turned toward her descending the stairs, she felt the weight of his attention like a physical thing.

"Assessor Thorne." His voice was crisp, professional. "Enforcer Tavian. I trust your evaluation is complete?"

"Indeed." Mira handed him the sealed report, her voice steady despite the treasonous lie burning in her chest. "Standard preservation enchantments, though somewhat elaborate. Nothing beyond Guild protocols."

Tavian took the report but didn't immediately open it. Instead, his pale gaze swept the foyer, lingering on the swaying chandelier, the weeping walls, the faint shimmer of temporal displacement that clung to the shadows.

"Strange magic here," he murmured, his eyes narrowing as he studied the walls as though they were whispering secrets. "You're sure the report's accurate, Assessor Thorne?"

For a heartbeat, Mira felt the weight of his suspicion like ice in her veins. But then she thought of Elara's sacrifice, of Corwin's faithful vigil, of love that had chosen transformation over destruction.

"Quite sure," she said, meeting his gaze without flinching. "Though I admit the temporal echoes are... pronounced. The family's attachment to this place has left deep impressions."

Tavian's expression didn't change, but something shifted in his posture—a subtle easing that suggested acceptance, if not complete belief. He tucked the report into his coat with efficient movements.

"Very well. The Guild thanks you for your service, Assessor Thorne. You're to report to headquarters for reassignment within the week."

He turned toward the door, then paused, glancing back over his shoulder. "Though I confess, I've rarely seen an estate quite so... responsive to emotion. The magic here feels almost alive."

Mira's heart stuttered, but she forced her expression to remain neutral. "Old houses often develop personality over time. It's not uncommon in preservation magic."

"No," Tavian agreed softly. "I suppose it isn't."

He left without another word, his boots clicking against the marble with military precision. Through the tall windows, Mira watched him mount his horse and ride away with his escort, taking her lie and their salvation back to Guild headquarters.

Only when the sound of hoofbeats had faded entirely did she allow herself to breathe.

The house sighed around her, its walls warm with approval, as the weight of what she'd done settled into her bones like a blessing and a burden in equal measure.

She had chosen love over law, protection over protocol.

CHAPTER 6

THE SPACE BETWEEN WORLDS

T hree days passed before Mira realized she had no intention of leaving.

She told herself it was professional thoroughness—that her falsified report required careful documentation to withstand future scrutiny, that she needed to understand the full scope of the preservation magic before departing. But the truth was simpler and more complicated: she had nowhere else she wanted to be.

The Guild would expect her return within the week, would assign her to another estate, another assessment, another careful cataloging of magical decay. The thought filled her with a bone-deep weariness she hadn't recognized until now. How many years had she spent reducing wonder to measurements, transforming mystery into mundane reports?

She had come here to measure magic like decay in a tomb. But what she'd found was birth—not of something new, but of something still becoming.

Here, at least, the mystery was allowed to remain mysterious.

She found Corwin in the morning parlor, seated at a small

table that definitely hadn't been there the day before. The house continued its subtle accommodations, reshaping itself around their needs with the gentle consideration of a perfect host. Today the room felt bright and welcoming, all cream silk and polished mahogany, with sunlight streaming through windows that showed a garden in full spring bloom despite the autumn chill outside.

"You're still here," he observed, not looking up from the letter he was writing. His handwriting was elegant, old-fashioned, the kind taught to aristocratic children generations ago.

"So are you," Mira replied, settling into the chair across from him. The house had provided tea again—the exact blend she preferred. She was beginning to suspect it knew her better than she knew herself.

Corwin's scars pulsed faintly, a rhythm she'd learned to read over the past few days. Contentment mixed with concern, like light filtered through colored glass. "I have an excuse for lingering. What's yours?"

The question was gentle, curious rather than challenging. Over the past three days, the sharp edges of his aristocratic mask had worn smooth, revealing glimpses of the man beneath—someone younger than his bearing suggested, marked by loss but not consumed by it.

"I'm writing supplementary documentation," Mira said, gesturing toward her journal. "In case the Guild requires additional information."

It was partially true. She had been writing, but not the kind of reports the Guild would recognize. Instead, she'd been documenting the small miracles she witnessed daily: the way the house hummed lullabies when Corwin couldn't sleep, how the mirrors reflected not just images but memories, the patterns of light that danced through the rooms like visible music.

Corwin's smile suggested he saw through her excuse as clearly as she did. "And how long will this... documentation require?"

Before she could answer, the air shimmered, and Elara materialized in the chair beside Corwin. She was more solid than ever, her presence carrying weight and warmth that made the furniture around her seem less substantial by comparison.

"As long as she needs," Elara said, reaching toward Corwin's hand. Her fingers passed through his, but both of them smiled as if the touch had been complete. "Time moves differently here, remember? A week could be a day, or a season, or a heartbeat."

Mira watched the interplay between them—love expressed through glances and almost-touches, conversation that carried layers of meaning . It was beautiful and heartbreaking in equal measure.

"The Guild will notice if I don't return," Mira said.

"Will they?" Elara's storm-gray eyes fixed on her with gentle intensity. "Or will they simply assume you've been delayed by the complexity of the assessment? Time is... flexible here. Your arrival three days ago could just as easily have been three hours, from their perspective."

The implications sent a chill through Mira. "You're talking about temporal manipulation. That's beyond preservation magic—it's reality alteration."

"Is it?" Corwin set down his pen, giving her his full attention. "Or is it simply that love creates its own physics? That the heart measures time differently than the clock?"

The room around them seemed to pulse with gentle

approval, and Mira felt the truth of it in her bones. She had lost track of time here, not through magical compulsion but through simple contentment. When had she last checked her pocket watch? When had she last counted the hours until departure?

But even as the thought comforted her, a distant sound made her pause—the faint echo of hoofbeats that seemed to come from somewhere outside time itself, a reminder that the world beyond these walls continued its relentless march forward.

"What are you asking me?" she said quietly.

Elara leaned forward, her translucent form blazing with earnest hope. "We're asking if you'd like to stay. Not forever— we understand that you have a life beyond these walls. But for a while. Long enough to document what we're becoming, to understand it fully."

"Long enough to help us figure out what comes next," Corwin added. "The binding between Elara and myself... it's evolving. Changing into something we don't have words for yet. We could use someone with your expertise to help us understand the implications."

Mira looked around the morning parlor, at the impossible beauty of the room , at two people who had refused to let death end their love story. She thought of Guild headquarters, of sterile offices and carefully regulated magic, of reports that reduced wonder to footnotes.

Time was flexible here, but the world outside wasn't. Eventually, that world would come calling.

"My expertise is in magical decay," she said. "Assessment and containment. What you're describing sounds more like... creation."

"Perhaps that's exactly what we need," Elara said softly. "Someone who understands how magic dies, to help us ensure this magic truly lives."

The letter Corwin had been writing drew her attention—elegant script covering cream paper with words she couldn't quite read from this angle. "What were you writing?" she asked.

Corwin's expression grew thoughtful. "A letter to my cousin in the capital. He's been handling the estate's legal affairs since... since Elara's death. I was explaining that the caretaker situation had become more permanent than originally planned."

"Your cousin believes you're the caretaker?"

"He believes Corwin Blackthorn died seven years ago in a magical accident," Elara said, her voice heavy with old sorrow. "Which, in a sense, he did. The man who bound himself to this house... he's something new. Something between what was and what could be."

Mira felt pieces clicking into place. "That's why you never gave your full name. You're not just any caretaker—you're family. Blackthorn family."

Corwin's scars flared brighter, and his smile held equal parts pain and dark amusement. "Guilty as charged. Corwin Blackthorn, wastrel second son, presumed dead and happier for it. Though I suppose that makes me something of a fraud—letting you believe I was merely hired help."

"You were protecting yourself," Mira said. "And her. If the Guild had known you were family, they would have investigated more thoroughly."

"Would they have discovered the truth?" Elara asked.

Mira considered this. "Possibly. Probably. Family members binding themselves to preservation magic... it's not unheard of, though it's illegal. But what you've accomplished here goes far beyond simple binding. This is..." She paused, searching for words. "This is love made manifest. Grief transformed into beauty. I don't think the Guild has protocols for that."

The admission hung in the air between them, weighted with possibility. Mira found herself thinking of her small apartment near Guild headquarters, of shelves lined with assessment reports that no one would ever read, of a life measured in magical regulations and careful distances.

When had she last felt truly useful? When had her work mattered beyond filing requirements and bureaucratic necessity?

"I could stay for a while," she said finally. "A few more days, perhaps a week. Long enough to document the evolution you're describing."

Elara's smile was radiant. "The house would be delighted to accommodate you longer."

As if summoned by her words, the room around them shimmered subtly. The walls shifted from cream to the softest blue, and new furniture appeared—a writing desk perfectly sized for Mira's needs, positioned to catch the morning light. Books materialized on shelves that hadn't existed moments before, volumes on magical theory and temporal enchantment that she'd only heard described in advanced courses.

"The house approves," Corwin said, his tone dry but fond. "It's been lonely, I think. Eager for some new perspective."

Mira rose from her chair and approached the new desk, running her fingers along its polished surface. The wood was warm beneath her touch, humming with a gentle magic that felt like welcome made tangible.

"What exactly am I documenting?" she asked.

"Everything," Elara said simply. "The daily miracles, the small impossibilities. The way love changes when it's no longer bound by mortality. The way magic evolves when it's fed by something stronger than mere will."

"Document us," Corwin added, his voice soft with something that might have been hope. "So that someday, when others find magic like this, they'll have a record of what's possible. A roadmap for transformation instead of destruction."

The weight of it settled on Mira's shoulders—not burden, but purpose. She was being asked to become more than an assessor, more than a cataloger of decay. She was being asked to become a chronicler of the impossible, a witness to love that had transcended every boundary the world recognized.

"I'll need to send word to the Guild," she said. "Explain the delay."

"Already taken care of," Elara said, her smile mysterious. "Time, remember? From their perspective, you've only just arrived. Your preliminary report bought us breathing room."

Mira nodded, though part of her wondered exactly how deep the temporal manipulation went here. Was she truly choosing to stay, or had the house's magic influenced her decision? Did it matter if the choice felt right?

She settled at the new desk, pulling out her journal and turning to a fresh page. At the top, she wrote: *Documentation of Magical Evolution: The Blackthorn Preservation Matrix.*

Below that, she added: *Day One of Extended Assessment.*

It felt like beginning a new chapter—not just in her documentation, but in her life. She was no longer just observing magic; she was becoming part of it, allowing it to change her as much as she studied its changes.

"Where do we begin?" she asked.

Corwin and Elara exchanged one of their wordless communications, the kind that spoke of understanding built across years and the boundary between life and death.

"With the truth," Elara said finally. "All of it. The curse that created us, the magic that sustains us, and the love that transforms us daily. No Guild protocols, no careful omissions. Just the story as it really happened."

"And as it continues to happen," Corwin added. "Because this isn't a preservation of the past, Miss Thorne. It's a creation of the future."

Mira dipped her pen in ink that seemed to shimmer with its own inner light—another gift from the accommodating house. As she prepared to write, she felt a shift in the air around her, a sense of doors opening that she hadn't known were closed.

For the first time in years, she was about to document something that mattered. Something that would change how magic was understood, how love was measured, and how the impossible was categorized.

She began to write, and the house hummed its approval around her like a lullaby.

CHAPTER 7

THE LANGUAGE OF BECOMING

T he first week dissolved into something that felt like months or perhaps minutes—time had become negotiable at Blackthorn Estate, flowing according to the rhythms of hearts rather than clocks. Mira found herself settling into patterns that should have felt strange but instead felt like coming home: morning tea with Corwin in whichever room the house deemed most suitable, afternoons documenting the small impossibilities that bloomed like flowers throughout the estate, evenings in the observatory watching Elara teach her the astronomy of memory.

Her Guild-issued timepiece had stopped working on the fourth day, its hands frozen at half-past three as if the mechanism had simply given up trying to measure something unmeasurable. She'd tucked it away without regret, learning instead to read time in the way Corwin's scars pulsed with the house's moods, the way Elara's form grew more solid when they spoke of the future.

The house itself had begun treating her less like a guest and more like family. Rooms rearranged themselves to accommodate her preferred lighting for writing. Books appeared on her shelves—first Guild texts she'd mentioned needing, then works on magical theory she'd never heard of, and finally volumes of poetry and philosophy that seemed chosen by someone who understood her thoughts better than she did.

"You're becoming part of it," Corwin observed one morning, finding her in what had once been the conservatory. The room had transformed itself overnight into something between a greenhouse and a library, with vines of silver growing between bookcases in impossible spirals.

Mira looked up from her notes, realizing he was right. The vines had grown around her chair while she worked, not restraining but embracing, their metallic leaves rustling with a sound like distant music. When she moved, they swayed aside to accommodate her, then reformed around her as if she belonged in their pattern.

"Is that dangerous?" she asked, though she felt no alarm. The vines' touch was warm, welcoming—like being held by something vast and patient.

"Only if you fight it," Elara said, materializing among the silver growth. Today she was so solid Mira could see her reflection in the greenhouse windows, her midnight blue gown seeming to absorb and redistribute the morning light. "The house has always been protective of those it loves."

Those it loves. The phrase settled into Mira's chest with unexpected warmth. When had she stopped being an intruder and become beloved? When had this impossible place begun to feel more real than the world beyond its walls?

"The Guild will expect contact soon," Mira said, though the words felt hollow even as she spoke them. "Enforcer Tavian's report will have reached headquarters by now. They'll want confirmation that the situation is contained."

The silver vines around her chair rustled with agitation,

their music turning discordant. Through the greenhouse glass, the garden beyond flickered between seasons—spring roses blooming while autumn leaves fell, winter frost touching summer hollyhocks.

"The house is distressed," Elara observed, her form flickering in response to the magical turbulence. "It doesn't like reminders of the outside world."

But isolation, however beautiful, couldn't last forever. The Guild had resources, patience, and an institutional memory that spanned centuries. Eventually, they would return.

"What happens when they come back?" she asked.

Corwin's scars dimmed, and for a moment, he looked achingly mortal—a man carrying a burden too heavy for human shoulders. "We face whatever comes. Together."

It was a non-answer that avoided the brutal mathematics of their situation. One Guild Enforcer could level this place if he understood what it truly was. A full investigation team would leave nothing but ash and carefully worded reports about the dangers of unregulated magic.

THE MESSAGE CRYSTAL'S departure left a strange hollowness in the air, as if the house itself mourned the connection to the outside world. Mira watched from the observatory's crystal dome as the magical construct flew north toward Guild headquarters, carrying her carefully crafted lies wrapped in official language.

Temporal disturbances affecting chronometric equipment. Extended documentation is required for unusual preservation matrices. Request an additional two weeks for a comprehensive assessment.

It would buy them time—perhaps a month if she was

fortunate. But this reprieve came with a cost: every lie she told deepened her complicity, made her more an enemy of the institution she'd served faithfully for years.

"Regrets?" Corwin asked, joining her at the observatory's edge where starlight painted impossible patterns across the crystal ceiling.

"Some," Mira admitted. "I've built my entire life around Guild service. Walking away from that... it's like discovering I've been speaking the wrong language all these years."

"And now?"

"Now I'm learning a new one." She gestured toward the flowing light that filled the observatory, the visible manifestation of love transcendent. "The language of becoming instead of cataloging. Of protection instead of assessment."

Elara materialized beside them, more radiant than ever in the starlight. Over the past days, her form had grown increasingly solid, her presence more anchored to the physical world. The evolution Corwin had spoken of was accelerating.

"The binding is changing," Elara said, following Mira's gaze to where light streamed between her translucent fingers. "Growing stronger, but also more... complex. I can feel Corwin's presence constantly now, like an echo of my own heartbeat."

Corwin's scars pulsed in response, their silver glow matching the rhythm of Elara's luminescence. "And I can feel yours. Sometimes I forget where I end and you begin."

The intimacy of it made Mira's breath catch. This was evolution in real time—two souls learning to exist as something larger than the sum of their parts. She reached for her journal, then stopped, her pen hovering over the page. How did one describe love that had learned to rewrite the rules of existence? How did one measure the immeasurable?

Instead, she watched as they moved closer together, the

air between them beginning to shimmer, reality bending around their proximity like heat waves rising from summer stone.

Their forms began to overlap—not physically, but magically, their essences intertwining in patterns that made Mira's trained eye water. She could see the binding threads that connected them, silver filaments that pulsed with shared heartbeats, carried shared thoughts.

"We call it confluence," Corwin said, his voice echoing strangely as if spoken from a great distance. "Moments when the boundary between us dissolves entirely."

"It's not always comfortable," Elara added, her words harmonizing with his in an impossible counterpoint. "The human mind isn't designed for dual consciousness. But it's beautiful," they finished together, their voices perfectly synchronized.

Mira felt tears prick her eyes as she watched them navigate this transformation with the grace of dancers learning new steps. But she could also see the cost etched in Corwin's increasingly translucent form, the way his mortality was slowly burning away like a candle in the wind.

"How long do you have? And are you afraid?" The questions came out in a rush, before she could soften them.

The confluence dissolved, leaving them separate again but somehow still connected by invisible threads. Corwin's hand moved unconsciously to his throat, fingers pressing against the scars that marked his deepening transformation.

"Months, perhaps. Maybe less." His honesty was stark, unadorned. "And yes, I'm afraid. Not of dying—that fear left me years ago. But of losing myself entirely. Of becoming so merged with Elara that Corwin simply... ceases to exist."

Elara reached toward him, her fingers stopping just short of his cheek. "You won't disappear. I won't let that happen."

"You may not have a choice. Love doesn't always preserve what we want to keep."

The words hung in the air like a challenge, and suddenly, Mira understood why her Guild timepiece had stopped. It wasn't just temporal displacement—it was her old worldview fracturing beyond repair, the careful measurements of her former life rendered meaningless by something too vast to quantify.

"What if there was another way?" she said suddenly, an idea crystallizing with startling clarity. "What if we could work with the Guild instead of hiding from them?"

Both of them turned toward her with expressions that mixed hope and horror.

"Hear me out," Mira continued, moving to the star charts that covered one wall of the observatory. "What if we presented this as research? A controlled study of magical evolution? The Guild is always interested in advancing theoretical knowledge."

"They're also terrified of anything they can't control," Elara pointed out.

"Then we make them believe they can control it." Mira's finger traced constellation patterns that seemed to shift and change as she watched. "We frame this as discovery, not rebellion. Make them partners in understanding instead of enemies of deviation."

The silence that followed was heavy with possibility and risk. Corwin's scars pulsed faster, and the house around them seemed to hold its breath.

"If they reject the proposal," Corwin said slowly, "they'll destroy everything. And you, along with us, for treason against Guild authority."

"If they accept it," Mira countered, "you might survive the transformation with your identity intact. You might become something unprecedented in magical history—together, but still yourselves."

"And if we do nothing?"

"Then Corwin could fade away by degrees, Elara exists alone in a house full of memories, and I become complicit in preserving something beautiful that slowly destroys itself."

The brutal arithmetic of their situation lay exposed between them. Each path carried the risk of total loss, but only one offered the possibility of guided transformation instead of helpless dissolution.

"Think about it," Mira said. "But don't take too long. Change is coming whether we guide it or not. The question is whether we want to face it alone or with allies who might actually be able to help."

As if summoned by her words, the stars visible through the crystal dome began to pulse in complex patterns, and the house around them hummed with anticipation.

The future was approaching, and it would demand choices from all of them.

Mira only hoped they would choose wisely enough to preserve what mattered most: not just love transcendent, but the individual souls who had chosen to transcend together.

In her pocket, the broken timepiece gave a single, impossible tick—as if time itself had decided to move forward again.

CHAPTER 8

THE ART OF DANGEROUS TRUTHS

T he Guild's response arrived at dawn, carried by a crystal construct that blazed through the morning mist like a falling star. Mira watched it streak toward the observatory from her position in the garden, where she'd been documenting the way roses bloomed and withered in impossible cycles, their petals shifting through seasons with each breath of wind.

The construct struck the crystal dome with a sound like thunder, then dissolved into words that hung in the air like accusations:

Assessment period concluded. Return to headquarters immediately for debriefing. Replacement assessor dispatched. Arrival expected within forty-eight hours. —Guild Master Aldric

Forty-eight hours. Less than she'd hoped for, more than she'd feared. But the mention of a replacement assessor sent ice through her veins. They weren't just recalling her—they were ensuring continuity of observation.

The house shuddered around them, its walls groaning with distress. Windows began fogging from the inside, and the roses at Mira's feet suddenly bloomed in violent profusion, their thorns growing longer and sharper as if preparing for battle.

"Not ideal timing," Corwin observed, appearing beside her with the fluid grace that marked his increasing transformation. This morning, he was almost translucent in the dawn light, his scars the only solid thing about him.

"No," Mira agreed, watching the message crystal's fragments fade to ash. "But perhaps it's the push we needed."

Over the past three days since she'd first proposed collaboration with the Guild, they'd debated the idea in circles. Elara favored caution, arguing for deeper concealment. Corwin vacillated between hope and terror. And Mira found herself caught between her professional instincts and her growing understanding that some things transcended institutional approval.

But now the choice was being forced upon them.

"The replacement assessor," she said, her mind racing through possibilities. "Who would they send?"

"Someone expendable," Corwin replied, his voice carrying the bitter wisdom of aristocratic experience. "Or someone they trust completely. Either way, not someone inclined toward... flexible interpretation of Guild protocols."

The house's distress was growing stronger. Through the conservatory windows, Mira could see furniture rearranging itself frantically, books reshuffling on shelves, mirrors reflecting scenes from decades past as if the estate were trying to retreat entirely into memory.

"Elara's frightened," Corwin murmured, his scars pulsing in rhythm with the house's agitation. "She's never faced Guild scrutiny while maintaining this level of consciousness. The risk..."

He didn't need to finish. If the new assessor discovered

the truth—if they possessed instruments capable of detecting life-force binding—the consequences would be immediate and final.

"Then we don't give them the chance to discover anything," Mira said, her resolve crystallizing into something harder than diamond. "We control the narrative from the beginning."

She turned toward the house, raising her voice to address the presence that dwelt within its walls. "Elara? I know you can hear me. We need to talk."

The air shimmered, and Elara materialized before them in a rush of light and anguish. Her form was more solid than ever, but also more unstable—flickering between states.

"They're coming," Elara whispered, her storm-gray eyes wide with fear. "I can feel them already, their intentions sharp as knives. They want to tear us apart."

"Not if we don't let them," Mira said firmly. "But we need to act quickly, and we need to act together."

She looked between Corwin and Elara, seeing love and terror warring in their expressions. Seven years of careful concealment were about to be tested against Guild scrutiny, and the margin for error had shrunk to nothing.

"I'm going to contact my supervisor directly," Mira continued. "Not Guild Master Aldric—he's too rigid, too bound by protocol. But Senior Assessor Thane. She's brilliant, pragmatic, and she understands that magic sometimes evolves beyond our current frameworks."

But even as she spoke, uncertainty gnawed at her. Thane had once overturned a Council decision to ban transmutation research—but she had also sanctioned the disbandment of three unregulated sanctuaries. Her pragmatism cut both ways, and there was no guarantee which edge would turn toward them.

"And if she doesn't listen?" Corwin asked.

"Then we face the alternative assessor with a united front and hope for the best." Mira's smile was sharp as broken glass. "But Thane will listen. She has to—because what we're offering is too valuable to ignore."

Elara's form flickered more violently, and her voice carried a note of raw terror. "They won't just test Corwin," she whispered. "They'll unmake me to see how I hold together. They'll dissect years of love like a specimen on a table."

The words struck Mira like a physical blow. In her calculations of political maneuvering, she'd momentarily forgotten the human cost—that Elara would bear the brunt of any Guild investigation, her very existence subject to scrutiny that could destroy her.

"That won't happen," Mira said fiercely. "I won't let it happen."

"Promises," Corwin said softly, "are dangerous things to make when dealing with institutional power."

SENIOR ASSESSOR LYDIA THANE was a woman who had built her reputation on impossible cases—magical anomalies that defied classification, enchantments that shouldn't work but did, and practitioners who pushed the boundaries of what the Guild considered safe or sane. If anyone in the organization would understand the potential value of Corwin and Elara's transformation, it would be her.

Mira composed her message with the care of a diplomat walking through a minefield:

Senior Assessor Thane—I write regarding a situation of unprecedented magical significance at the Blackthorn Estate. Standard assessment protocols are inadequate for what I've discovered here. Request emergency consultation before replacement assessor arrives. The implications for Guild magical theory are... extraordinary.

—Assessor Thorne

She sealed the message in a priority crystal—the kind reserved for discoveries that could reshape magical understanding—and launched it toward the capital with hands that barely trembled.

Now came the waiting.

"Will she come?" Elara asked, her form pacing restlessly through the conservatory's silver vines.

"She'll come," Mira said with more confidence than she felt. "Thane's curiosity is stronger than her caution. If she thinks there's genuine discovery to be made..."

"And if the replacement assessor arrives first?"

That was the nightmare scenario—a by-the-books evaluator stumbling into a situation that required delicate handling, finding evidence of life-force binding, and responding with standard Guild protocols. Containment. Interrogation. Dismantlement.

"Then we improvise," Mira said. "But let's assume Thane responds quickly. She usually does."

Corwin had been silent throughout this exchange, his attention fixed on something beyond the conservatory windows. Now he spoke, his voice heavy with resignation.

"There's something you need to understand about Guild discovery protocols," he said. "I've studied them extensively over the years, preparing for this possibility. When they find magic like ours—magic that challenges fundamental assumptions about life and death—they don't just study it. They control it."

"What do you mean?"

"I mean, they'll want to replicate it. If the binding between

Elara and myself proves stable, if our transformation offers insights into consciousness preservation..." He turned toward them, his gray eyes bleak. "We won't be collaborators. We'll be specimens."

The words hit Mira like ice water. In her eagerness to find a diplomatic solution, she'd overlooked the most basic truth about Guild operations: they were collectors first, scholars second. Any magical phenomenon of sufficient interest became Guild property, its practitioners subject to whatever oversight the organization deemed necessary.

"They can't force participation in research," she said, though even as she spoke, she knew how naive the words sounded.

"Can't they?" Corwin's smile was bitter. "We're practitioners of illegal magic, Mira. Life-force binding is prohibited under Guild law. The moment they confirm what we are, we become criminals subject to Guild justice."

"Which means imprisonment at best," Elara added softly, her form flickering with each word. "Execution at worst."

The weight of what they were contemplating settled on Mira's shoulders like a stone. She'd been thinking like an academic, excited by the possibility of expanding magical knowledge. But Corwin was right—they were criminals in the eyes of Guild law, and criminals had no rights when it came to magical research.

"So we make sure they see us as something else," she said finally. "Not criminals. Not specimens. Partners."

"How?"

Mira moved to her writing desk, pulling out paper and ink. As she did, her fingers brushed against the broken Guild timepiece in her pocket—its stopped hands a reminder of how completely her old world had crumbled. The woman who had arrived here three weeks ago would never have contemplated what she was about to propose.

"By offering them something they want more than specimens. By making ourselves indispensable rather than merely interesting."

She began to write rapidly, her mind racing through possibilities. The Guild's greatest weakness was also its greatest strength: institutional conservatism. They feared change, but they also craved knowledge that would cement their authority over magical practice.

What if she could offer them both? A controlled study that expanded their understanding while posing no threat to their power structure?

"I'm going to propose a formal research partnership," she said, her pen scratching across the paper. "Sanctioned by Guild authority, conducted under Guild oversight, with results shared openly with the magical community. We become the first official study of consciousness preservation magic."

"And if they refuse?"

"Then we're no worse off than before." Mira looked up from her writing, meeting their worried gazes. "But if they accept... we become legitimate. Protected. Pioneers instead of criminals."

It was audacious, dangerous—the kind of gamble that could transform persecution into partnership or guarantee their destruction. But as Mira watched Corwin's fading solidity and Elara's desperate hope, she realized they were past the point of safe choices.

"There's something else," she continued, her voice dropping to a whisper. "If we can prove that love-based consciousness preservation is stable, replicable... the Guild will want to understand how to control it. They'll see potential applications for their own purposes."

"Applications like what?" Elara asked, though her voice suggested she already suspected the answer.

"Preserving their greatest minds beyond normal lifespans. Maintaining institutional memory through magical means. Creating advisors who can't be corrupted, coerced, or killed." Mira's smile was sharp with possibility and bitter with self-awareness. "They'll see you not as threats but as the key to their own immortality."

The conservatory fell silent as the implications sank in. They were talking about offering the Guild something it had never possessed: victory over death itself, wrapped in the promise of controlled study and institutional benefit.

It was either the most brilliant negotiation in Guild history or the most spectacular betrayal of everything Mira had ever believed in.

"Will you do it?" she asked them. "Will you trust me to speak for you?"

Corwin and Elara exchanged one of their wordless communications, love flowing between them in currents of silver light. Finally, Corwin nodded.

"We'll trust you," he said. "But understand—if this goes wrong, if they decide we're too dangerous to preserve..."

"I know." Mira sealed her proposal in another priority crystal, this one addressed directly to Guild Master Aldric himself. The broken timepiece seemed to pulse against her ribs, marking time that had already run out. "But we're out of safe choices. Now we find out if love can learn to speak the language of power."

As the crystal streaked away toward the capital, carrying their future in its crystalline heart, the house around them hummed with anticipation.

In less than forty-eight hours, they would discover whether magic could be both transcendent and practical, whether love could survive bureaucracy, whether three people who had learned to exist beyond normal boundaries could convince an institution to expand its definition of the possible.

The gamble was cast. Now came the most dangerous part: waiting to see how the dice would fall.

CHAPTER 9
THE WEIGHT OF INSTITUTIONAL POWER

T
he response arrived not as a crystal message but as a carriage—black lacquered wood bearing Guild crests, drawn by horses whose breath steamed silver in the morning air. Through the conservatory windows, Mira watched the procession approach with a mixture of relief and terror.

Senior Assessor Thane had come personally.

That could mean salvation or condemnation, and there was no way to know which until the woman stepped down from her carriage and spoke her first words.

"She's here," Mira called to Corwin, who materialized beside her with the fluid grace that marked his deepening transformation. This morning, he was barely more than a suggestion of light and memory, his scars the only solid thing about him.

"Impressive response time," he observed, though his voice carried undertones of dread. "Either she's very interested or very alarmed."

Through their bond, Elara's presence pressed against the edges of Mira's awareness—fear and hope tangled together like thorned vines. The house itself seemed to hold its breath, its magical signatures muted to barely detectable whispers.

They had agreed on a strategy during the sleepless hours before dawn: present themselves as researchers rather than refugees, frame their transformation as discovery rather than deviation. But strategies were fragile things when faced with institutional power.

Senior Assessor Lydia Thane was a woman who commanded attention without effort—tall and elegant, her silver hair pulled back in a style that suggested authority tempered by intelligence. She wore traveling robes of deep blue marked with Guild honors, and when she looked up at the conservatory windows, Mira felt the weight of a mind that missed nothing.

"Showtime," Mira murmured, straightening her own robes. The Guild insignia felt heavier than usual, weighted with the knowledge that she might be wearing it for the last time.

By the time Thane reached the front entrance, Mira was waiting in the foyer with carefully rehearsed composure. The house had cooperated beautifully, presenting its most benign face—no weeping walls, no temporal disturbances, just the refined elegance of a well-maintained estate.

"Senior Assessor Thane," Mira said, offering a precise bow. "Thank you for responding so quickly to my message."

"Assessor Thorne." Thane's voice carried the crisp authority of someone accustomed to being obeyed. "Your communication was... intriguing. Unprecedented magical significance, extraordinary implications for Guild theory." Her gray eyes swept the foyer, noting details with clinical precision. "I confess myself curious."

"The phenomenon is best observed rather than described,"

Mira replied, gesturing toward the grand staircase. "If you would permit me to demonstrate—"

"Before we proceed," Thane interrupted, her tone sharpening, "I should mention that Guild Master Aldric was... displeased by your request for extended assessment time. There are questions about your objectivity in this matter."

The words struck like a blade, but Mira forced her expression to remain neutral. "I understand the Guild's concerns. However, I believe you'll find that the situation warrants extraordinary measures."

"We shall see." Thane's smile was polite as winter frost. "Lead on, Assessor Thorne. Show me these unprecedented implications."

The morning parlor had arranged itself perfectly for their purposes—sunlight streaming through windows that showed only the present moment, furniture positioned to suggest comfort without excess. Corwin waited by the fireplace, solid enough to pass casual inspection but translucent enough to suggest something beyond normal human parameters.

"Senior Assessor Thane," Mira said formally, "may I present Corwin Blackthorn, caretaker of the estate and... our primary subject of study."

Corwin offered a bow that managed to be both respectful and slightly mocking. "Senior Assessor. Welcome to our home."

Thane's eyes narrowed as she studied him, her gaze lingering on the silver scars that traced his jaw and throat. "Fascinating. Magical scarring, but not from injury. These appear to be... integration marks?"

"Very astute," Corwin replied. "I confess myself impressed by your immediate recognition."

"I've seen similar patterns in advanced transmutation research, though never so extensive." Thane moved closer, her expression shifting from polite interest to genuine fascination. "The scarring suggests a deep magical transformation. How long has the process been ongoing?"

"Seven years," Mira answered. "Which brings us to the truly extraordinary aspect of this situation."

The air shimmered, and Elara materialized beside Corwin with the gradual grace of dawn breaking. She appeared exactly as they had planned—solid enough to be undeniably present, translucent enough to suggest magical preservation, beautiful enough to take Thane's breath away.

"Senior Assessor Thane," Elara said, her voice carrying the cultivated authority of nobility, "how lovely to have a guest who appreciates the subtleties of magical scholarship."

Thane went absolutely still. For a long moment, the only sound in the room was the gentle ticking of a clock that definitely hadn't been there moments before. When she finally spoke, her voice carried a note Mira had never heard from a Guild official: wonder.

"Consciousness preservation," Thane breathed. "Actual, stable consciousness preservation. Not just memory echoes or spiritual imprints, but full cognitive retention and environmental interaction."

"Indeed," Elara replied with a smile that mixed triumph and terror in equal measure. "Though the process has proven rather more complex than traditional theories would suggest."

Thane began circling them slowly, her trained eye cataloging details with the precision of a master craftsman examining a work of art.

"The energy signatures are unprecedented. Life-force preservation magic, but evolved beyond anything in Guild records. How did you achieve stability without catastrophic degradation?"

Mira felt her heart hammering against her ribs. This was

the crucial moment—Thane's response would determine whether they faced partnership or prosecution.

"That," Mira said carefully, "is where the research partnership becomes invaluable. What we've discovered here challenges fundamental assumptions about consciousness, magical integration, and the boundaries between life and death. But it requires careful study to understand the mechanisms involved."

"Research partnership?" Thane's eyebrow arched with dangerous interest.

As Mira pulled out her proposal, she caught sight of Corwin and Elara in her peripheral vision. While Thane examined the document, Corwin's hand moved unconsciously toward Elara's—not quite touching, but close enough that their magical signatures began to harmonize. The simple gesture sent silver light dancing between their fingertips, and Elara's translucent form steadied, becoming more solid in response to his proximity.

It lasted only a heartbeat before they both seemed to remember their audience and carefully separated. Condensed into wordless communication. *I'm here,* the gesture said. *Whatever comes, I'm here.*

The sight made her chest tighten with something that might have been envy. When had anyone ever reached for her like that—instinctively, protectively, as if her presence alone could steady their world?

"A formal collaboration between the Guild and the Blackthorn Estate," Mira continued, pulling out the proposal she'd crafted during the sleepless pre-dawn hours. "Sanctioned magical research into consciousness preservation, conducted under Guild oversight with full documentation and shared results."

She held her breath as Thane took the document,

watching the woman's expression shift as she read. Calculation, recognition, and something that might have been hunger flickered across her features.

"You're proposing to make test subjects of yourselves," Thane said finally. "To submit to Guild study in exchange for legal protection."

"We're proposing to advance magical understanding in areas that have been theoretically impossible," Corwin corrected, his voice steady despite the way his form flickered with tension. "The preservation matrix we've achieved here isn't just personal—it's replicable, with proper understanding."

The word 'replicable' hung in the air like a promise and a threat. Mira watched Thane's expression shift again, saw the moment when academic interest transformed into institutional desire.

"The applications," Thane murmured, almost to herself. "Knowledge preservation, advisory functions, institutional memory..." She looked up sharply. "You understand the implications of what you're suggesting?"

"We understand that the Guild values practical applications over theoretical purity," Elara said smoothly. "And we understand that cooperation serves everyone's interests better than confrontation."

It was a careful dance of words, each phrase chosen to suggest collaboration while avoiding the harsher realities they all understood. The Guild would never simply observe—they would want to control, replicate, and ultimately own whatever they discovered here.

But ownership was a negotiable concept, and partnership offered protections that rebellion never could.

"There are significant legal complications," Thane said, setting down the proposal. "Life-force binding is explicitly prohibited under Guild statute. What you've achieved here, regardless of its theoretical value, constitutes a clear violation of magical law."

"Which is why we need Guild partnership rather than Guild opposition," Mira replied. "Legal complications can be addressed through proper channels if the research is officially sanctioned."

"And if it's not?"

The unspoken threat underlay every word. They all knew what happened to unsanctioned magical research—containment, interrogation, disposal. The Guild's authority rested on its ability to control dangerous magic, and they had never hesitated to use that authority when threatened.

"If it's not," Corwin said quietly, "then you lose the chance to understand something that could revolutionize Guild operations. How many of your greatest minds have been lost to natural death? How many institutional secrets died with their keepers?"

Thane's eyes glittered with interest. "You're suggesting this preservation technique could be applied to Guild leadership."

"I'm suggesting that the possibilities are worth exploring," Corwin replied. "Under proper supervision, of course."

The calculation in Thane's expression was almost visible —weighing potential benefits against institutional risks, academic curiosity against regulatory duty. Mira found herself holding her breath, knowing that everything hung on this moment of decision.

"I would need guarantees," Thane said finally. "Complete cooperation with Guild oversight. Full documentation of all processes and techniques. And absolute commitment to Guild authority in all matters of research direction."

"Agreed," Mira said, the word feeling both like salvation

and surrender. "Though I assume the Guild would also commit to treating this as legitimate research rather than criminal investigation."

As she spoke, she noticed Elara's hand drift toward Corwin's throat, her translucent fingers hovering just above the silver scars that marked his transformation. She didn't touch—couldn't, with Thane watching—but Corwin's breathing deepened as if he could feel the phantom caress anyway. His scars pulsed once, brightly, in what looked like gratitude for comfort offered even when touch was impossible.

The micro-gesture spoke of intimacy so complete it transcended physical contact, love that had learned to communicate in frequencies no Guild instrument could detect.

It was capitulation disguised as negotiation, but it was also survival. Mira hesitated just long enough to feel the edges of regret press against her ribs. But there was no better offer coming. Not in this world.

Through their bond, she felt Elara's presence solidify with resolution. "I'd rather be studied than erased," Elara said quietly, her voice carrying the weight of seven years' worth of existence hanging in the balance. "If that's the price of being seen, then let them see me."

The simple honesty of it made Mira's chest tighten. Here was someone who had already sacrificed everything for love, now willing to sacrifice even more for survival.

"I believe we can reach mutually beneficial arrangements," Thane replied with a smile that promised nothing.

The house around them seemed to exhale with relief, though Mira noticed the walls had gone perfectly still—no gentle breathing motion, no subtle shifts in texture. Even the silver vines in the conservatory had drawn back into themselves, their music faded to silence. The estate itself understood what had just been lost.

"Excellent," Thane continued, pulling out a message crystal that pulsed with official authority. "I'll contact Guild Master Aldric immediately. We'll need a full research team here within the month—specialists in consciousness magic, preservation theory, and legal documentation."

As she began composing her message, Mira caught Corwin's eye. His expression mixed gratitude with resignation, understanding with regret. They had chosen survival, but survival came with chains—golden chains, perhaps, but chains nonetheless.

Elara's presence pressed against her awareness, carrying wordless communication that felt like acceptance and sorrow intertwined. They would live, would continue their transformation under Guild protection.

But they would never again be free to determine their own fate.

The message crystal blazed to life and streaked away toward the capital, carrying news that would transform the Blackthorn Estate from a hidden sanctuary into an official Guild research facility.

Mira watched it disappear into the morning sky and wondered if they had won salvation or simply chosen a more comfortable form of imprisonment.

CHAPTER 10

THE PRICE OF PROTECTION

The Guild research team arrived like an invasion disguised as scholarship.

Three carriages rolled through the estate gates at precisely noon, their black lacquer gleaming with protective wards that made Mira's teeth ache. Behind them came a supply wagon loaded with crystalline instruments that hummed with contained magic, their harmonic frequencies setting the house's windows to vibrating in distressed counterpoint.

Mira watched from the observatory's crystal dome as uniformed figures emerged from the carriages—six researchers, two guards, and Senior Assessor Thane herself, directing the operation with military precision. They moved across the grounds like pieces on a chess board, each knowing their role in the game to come.

"Impressive efficiency," Corwin observed, materializing beside her. His form was more translucent than ever, as if the approaching scrutiny were already beginning to wear him thin. "Though I notice they've brought guards to a research expedition."

"Standard protocol," Mira replied, though her voice carried little conviction. "The Guild takes no chances with potentially dangerous magic."

Below them, the house began to react to the invasion. Doors slammed shut of their own accord, only to swing open again when the researchers approached. Windows fogged and cleared in agitated cycles. The front garden's roses bloomed and withered in rapid succession, their petals falling like snow across the manicured paths.

Mira watched the systematic suppression of everything that made this place magical, and found herself thinking about her own carefully constructed life. She'd built career success by maintaining professional boundaries, by never getting too close to the magic she studied or the people who practiced it. But witnessing the Guild strip away the house's capacity for joy, watching researchers reduce years of devotion to clinical data points, she realized that her own isolation wasn't protection—it was its own form of preservation spell, keeping her safely separate from anything that might transform her.

When Thomas Whitmore had written from the southern territories five years ago, asking if she might consider a change of assignment, she'd filed his letter with professional correspondence and never replied. Geographic complications, she'd reasoned. Career implications. Now those reasons felt as hollow as the suppression fields trying to contain love that operated beyond measurement.

But it was the taste that hit Mira first—metallic and bitter, like blood mixed with winter air. The house's distress carried flavor, scent, temperature that had nothing to do with the physical world. Her breath misted despite the warmth of the day, and for a moment the observatory walls seemed to lean inward, as if seeking shelter from the approaching storm.

Elara appeared beside them, her form blazing with anxiety. "They're already testing," she said, her voice tight with strain.

Through their bond, Elara's presence pressed against the edges of Mira's awareness—fear and hope tangled together like thorned vines. But beneath the distress, she felt something else: the steady pulse of Corwin's consciousness reaching for Elara's across the suppression fields, a rhythmic reassurance that spoke louder than words.

Still here, his magical signature seemed to whisper. *Still choosing you.*

And Elara's response, faint but determined: *Still us. Still worth protecting.*

The silent conversation made Mira's throat tighten. Even under Guild suppression, even facing institutional dismantlement, they were more concerned with reassuring each other than protecting themselves.

"I can feel their instruments probing the estate's defenses, mapping the magical flows."

Thane had positioned her team in a careful perimeter around the house, each researcher activating crystalline detection devices that cast harsh blue light across the grounds. The instruments sang in discordant harmony, their frequencies designed to pierce through magical concealment and reveal the truth beneath.

"They'll find everything," Elara whispered, her form flickering like a candle in the wind. "Every secret, every hidden room, every moment of preserved memory."

Mira felt the weight of what they'd agreed to settle on her shoulders like a lead cloak. Complete cooperation. Full documentation. Absolute commitment to Guild authority. The words had seemed reasonable in the parlor's civilized atmosphere, but watching Thane's team deploy with clinical efficiency, she understood the true scope of what they'd surrendered.

For a heartbeat, she remembered her first morning here— sitting in the conservatory with Corwin, watching him trace patterns in spilled sugar while Elara laughed at something only they could hear. The intimacy of it, the precious ordinariness of love existing outside of time and regulation. Now it would all be measured, catalogued, and reduced to data points in Guild archives.

"We should go down," she said finally. "Meet them as partners, not subjects under observation."

But even as they descended the stairs, Mira could feel the house's distress growing. The walls themselves seemed to press inward, as if trying to hide from the probing instruments. Portraits along the hallway flickered between time periods, showing generations of Blackthorns in states of increasing agitation.

The foyer had arranged itself into a formal receiving room, though the crystalline chandelier swayed with nervous energy despite the absence of any breeze. Thane stood at the center of it all, consulting a device that mapped magical currents in three-dimensional light.

"Assessor Thorne," she said without looking up. "Perfect timing. We're just completing our preliminary survey."

"Finding anything interesting?" Mira asked, forcing her tone to remain casual.

"Fascinating would be more accurate." Thane finally raised her eyes from the device, and her expression held the hungry satisfaction of a predator that had found prey. "The magical saturation here is unlike anything in Guild records. The entire structure is suffused with preserved consciousness —not just in isolated pockets, but woven through every beam and stone."

Corwin's scars pulsed brighter, and Mira felt rather than saw Elara's presence draw closer, seeking comfort in proximity.

"The preservation matrix is remarkably stable," continued Dr. Helena Voss, a stern woman with iron-gray hair who had emerged from examining the eastern wing. Her instruments gleamed with the satisfaction of discoveries made, though something flickered across her expression when she looked at Elara—a moment of what might have been envy before professional detachment reasserted itself. "No degradation, no reality fractures, no temporal instabilities. It's as if the consciousness binding has achieved perfect equilibrium with the physical structure."

"Impossible under current theoretical frameworks," added Dr. Marcus Erisen, a younger man whose eager expression suggested this was the discovery that would make his career. But his enthusiasm wavered slightly when Corwin's gaze met his, and his next words came more quietly. "The energy requirements alone should have caused catastrophic failure within months, not sustained stability for years."

"The binding signatures are particularly intriguing," Dr. Voss continued, adjusting her instruments to focus on Corwin. "A dual-matrix preservation spell, anchored through willing sacrifice rather than forced extraction."

As she spoke, Corwin's gaze found Elara across the foyer. Despite the clinical discussion reducing their love to theoretical frameworks, his expression softened with the same wonder Mira had witnessed that first morning in the music room—as if seeing Elara still surprised him with joy, even after seven years of preservation magic.

Elara smiled in return, and for just a moment, her translucent form blazed brighter, responding to his attention like a flower turning toward sunlight. The simple exchange carried more warmth than any words could convey: *You're still beautiful to me. You're still everything.*

Dr. Voss, absorbed in her readings, missed the interplay entirely. But Mira caught it, and the casual intimacy—love persisting in the face of clinical observation—made her chest ache with recognition of something she'd never experienced herself.

They spoke of Elara as if she weren't there, reducing her to theoretical frameworks and energy equations. Mira felt anger kindle in her chest, but Corwin's hand—barely substantial though it was—pressed against her arm in warning.

Not yet, his touch seemed to say. *Let them reveal themselves first.*

"The binding signatures are particularly intriguing," Dr. Voss continued, adjusting her instruments to focus on Corwin. "A dual-matrix preservation spell, anchored through willing sacrifice rather than forced extraction. The scarring patterns suggest gradual integration over the years rather than a sudden transformation."

"Which raises questions about replicability," Thane observed, her tone carrying the weight of institutional planning. "If the process requires such extended timeframes, its practical applications may be limited."

"Unless," Dr. Erisen interjected, his eyes bright with possibility, "we can identify the key factors that enable acceleration. With proper understanding of the consciousness-transfer mechanisms—"

"You speak of us as though we're equations to be solved," Elara said suddenly, her voice cutting through their academic discourse like a blade. Her form solidified with anger, becoming more present and powerful than Mira had ever seen her. "Rather than people who chose transformation freely."

The research team went silent, their instruments still humming but their attention suddenly focused on the woman who had materialized before them like a challenge made manifest.

Dr. Voss recovered first, her expression shifting to professional courtesy tinged with barely concealed hunger. "Lady Blackthorn, I presume. Your preservation is indeed remarkable—consciousness retention appears complete, with a full personality matrix intact. We're eager to understand the mechanisms that enable such unprecedented stability."

"Understanding," Elara repeated, her storm-gray eyes glittering with dangerous light. "And what form will this understanding take? Observation? Experimentation? Vivisection?"

"Careful study," Thane interjected smoothly. "Non-invasive analysis, consciousness mapping, energy flow documentation. We're researchers, not barbarians."

But Mira caught the way Dr. Erisen's fingers caressed a crystalline probe that pulsed with extraction frequencies, the way Dr. Voss's instruments remained focused on Corwin despite the polite conversation. These were people who saw breakthrough discoveries rather than sentient beings.

"The research protocols are quite comprehensive," Thane continued, pulling out a scroll that unrolled to reveal pages of densely written procedures. "Daily consciousness mapping, weekly energy analysis, monthly preservation matrix evaluation. We'll need complete access to all aspects of the binding —personal histories, emotional resonances, the specific circumstances that enabled the initial transformation."

"Complete access," Corwin said quietly, his voice carrying a note of dark amusement. "How thorough of you."

"Thoroughness is essential for proper documentation," Dr. Voss replied, missing or ignoring the warning in his tone.

"We'll need to understand every variable that contributed to your transformation's success. Personal relationships, emotional states, the precise magical techniques employed—"

"Our love story as a case study," Elara murmured, her form flickering with something that might have been humor or despair. "How romantic."

The house around them shuddered, and for a moment, the walls showed their true nature—stone, and timber suffused with silver light, every surface alive with preserved memory and emotion. The Guild instruments shrieked in harmony as their readings spiked beyond measurement.

"Extraordinary," Dr. Erisen breathed, his devices glowing so brightly they cast harsh shadows across his eager face. "The emotional resonance is off the charts. The consciousness preservation appears to be linked to intense affective states—"

"Love," Mira said flatly. "The word you're avoiding is love."

"Emotional attachment," Dr. Voss corrected with clinical precision. "Strong psychological bonds that create stable energy matrices for consciousness anchoring. The specific nature of the attachment is less relevant than its intensity and duration."

Mira felt something cold settle in her stomach. "I see," Elara said softly, her voice carrying the chill of aristocratic displeasure. "We are to be your laboratory rats, then. Observed, measured, and cataloged for the advancement of Guild knowledge."

"You are to be our partners," Thane corrected, though her tone suggested the partnership would be distinctly unequal. "Protected under Guild authority, supported by Guild resources, and remembered as pioneers who expanded the boundaries of magical understanding."

"And if we object to certain aspects of the research?"

Thane's smile was sharp as winter ice. "I'm sure that won't be necessary. After all, you've already agreed to complete cooperation."

The words hung in the air like a trap closing, and Mira realized with crystalline clarity that they had indeed agreed to this—had volunteered for it, even. In their desperation to avoid destruction, they had chosen a more civilized form of imprisonment.

But imprisonment nonetheless.

"Perhaps," Corwin said, his scars blazing brighter as his form began to fade, "we should discuss the specific terms of this cooperation. In private."

"I'm afraid that won't be possible," Dr. Voss replied, her instruments tracking his every flicker. "The research requires continuous observation to capture all stages of the consciousness evolution. Privacy would compromise data integrity."

"Continuous observation," Elara repeated, her voice flat with dawning horror.

Beside her, Corwin's form flickered with distress, but not for himself. His attention was entirely on Elara, watching the way her shoulders tensed as the full scope of their situation became clear. Without thinking, he took a half-step closer— not touching, but positioning himself so that his presence formed a shield between her and the Guild researchers' hungry stares.

The protective gesture was so automatic it seemed unconscious, expressing itself in body language that spoke of someone who would always, always step between his beloved and harm. Elara's translucent form steadied in response to his proximity, drawing strength from his willingness to be her sanctuary even when he had no power to actually protect her.

Watching them, Mira realized she was witnessing love at its most essential—not the grand gestures or passionate declarations, but the quiet choice to be someone's refuge, again and again, in whatever small ways remained possible.

"Continuous observation," Elara repeated.

"Standard protocol for phenomena of this significance," Thane said smoothly. "Though we'll naturally provide reasonable accommodations for personal comfort."

Mira looked around the foyer, seeing it with new eyes. The Guild team had already begun setting up their equipment—crystalline monitoring devices in every corner, detection grids that would map every magical fluctuation, recording instruments that would capture every word, every gesture, every moment of intimacy between two souls who had already sacrificed everything for love.

They had escaped the Guild's initial judgment only to face something worse: institutionalized voyeurism disguised as scholarship.

"The house objects," Corwin said suddenly, his voice carrying an odd harmonic as the walls around them began to groan with stress. "It doesn't like strangers. Particularly strangers with intrusive intentions."

As if summoned by his words, the Guild instruments began to malfunction. Crystalline recording devices cracked under sudden pressure. Detection grids flickered and died. Dr. Erisen's consciousness mapping apparatus exploded in a shower of sparks that left him singed and speechless.

"Fascinating," Dr. Voss murmured, apparently unperturbed by the magical rebellion erupting around her. "Defensive responses integrated into the preservation matrix. The consciousness isn't just preserved—it's protective."

"Stand down," Thane commanded, her voice cracking with authority. "Estate defenses will not be permitted to interfere with Guild research."

She raised her own device—a crystalline rod that pulsed

with suppression frequencies designed to dampen hostile magic. The house's rebellion immediately began to fade, its walls falling still, its protests silenced by institutional power.

Elara's form flickered wildly, her connection to the estate's magic disrupted by Thane's intervention. "Stop," she gasped, her voice growing faint. "You're severing the bonds—"

"Temporarily," Thane replied with clinical detachment. "Magical suppression is necessary for researcher safety. The effects will dissipate once the estate accepts our presence."

But Mira could see the cost written in Corwin's increasingly translucent form, in Elara's desperate struggle to maintain coherence. The suppression wasn't just dampening the house's defenses—it was attacking the very foundations of their preserved existence.

"You're killing them," Mira said, her voice sharp with alarm.

"We're establishing proper research parameters," Dr. Voss corrected. "Initial discomfort is normal when consciousness preservation matrices are subjected to external regulation."

External regulation. The phrase sent ice through Mira's veins. They weren't just studying Corwin and Elara—they were actively controlling them, reducing them to subjects whose very existence could be modulated at Guild discretion.

"The suppression will be reduced as cooperation improves," Thane said, lowering her device.

As the magical dampening eased slightly, Corwin's scars pulsed once in what looked like relief. But his first instinct wasn't self-preservation—it was to turn toward Elara, checking her stability before his own. She was watching him with the same concern, her storm-gray eyes cataloging the cost the suppression had taken on his increasingly translucent form.

Their silent assessment of each other's well-being, the

way they prioritized the other's suffering over their own, spoke of love that had been tested by seven years of impossible circumstances and emerged stronger for it.

In that moment, Mira understood exactly why she'd risked everything to protect them. This wasn't just magical preservation—it was proof that love could transcend every boundary the world imposed, that some connections were too precious to be reduced to research parameters.

The silence that followed was deafening—not just the absence of sound, but the absence of life itself. For a heartbeat, the house felt truly dead, its magical voice strangled into nothing. Then, gradually, some strength returned to Elara's form, though she remained pale and trembling.

"We're not monsters, Assessor Thorne," Thane continued after the weighted pause. "We simply require compliance with research protocols."

Compliance. Cooperation. Research parameters. Each word was chosen to obscure the fundamental truth: they had traded freedom for survival, only to discover that survival under Guild protection was indistinguishable from exquisitely polite torture.

"Now then," Thane continued, her tone returning to professional courtesy, "shall we begin the formal documentation process? Dr. Erisen will handle consciousness mapping, Dr. Voss will analyze the preservation matrices, and I'll oversee emotional resonance evaluation."

She turned toward Corwin and Elara with the satisfaction of someone who had acquired valuable specimens. "We have such fascinating work ahead of us."

Mira watched the Guild researchers deploy their instruments with practiced efficiency, transforming the foyer into a laboratory where love would be dissected with clinical precision. The house around them had fallen silent, its magical voice muted by suppression fields that turned a home into a prison.

They had chosen this. Had volunteered for it. Had signed documents agreeing to complete cooperation with Guild authority.

But as she watched Corwin's form flicker under the harsh light of monitoring devices, as she saw Elara struggle to maintain coherence while surrounded by instruments designed to measure her soul, Mira realized that some choices were made not from wisdom but from the absence of alternatives.

The Guild had offered protection, and they had accepted.

Now they would discover what protection truly cost.

The real research was about to begin—and Mira suspected none of them would emerge unchanged from what the Guild considered necessary for the advancement of magical knowledge.

In the corner of her vision, she caught sight of her reflection in one of the foyer's mirrors. The woman looking back at her wore Guild robes and carried Guild authority, but her eyes held the hollow recognition of someone who had chosen collaboration over courage.

The worst part was knowing that even now, with the true nature of their bargain revealed, there was still no better choice available.

They would endure. They would cooperate. They would submit to whatever the Guild deemed necessary.

CHAPTER 11

THE ARCHITECTURE OF RESISTANCE

T
he first week of Guild observation passed like a fever dream measured in crystalline monitoring frequencies and documented emotional responses.

Mira woke each morning to silence where music once lived. No longer did the house hum lullabies through the walls, no longer did breakfast appear perfectly prepared on tables that materialized with thoughtful care. The suppression fields had stripped away more than magic—they had stolen the estate's voice, its breath, the gentle rustle of fabric that spoke of rooms rearranging themselves with joy. Even the air felt different, flat and lifeless, lacking the subtle perfume of roses that had once drifted through every corridor like captured summer.

She found Corwin in the morning parlor, though "found" was perhaps too generous a term. The Guild researchers had established a rigid schedule: consciousness mapping from eight to ten, preservation matrix analysis until noon, and emotional resonance evaluation through the afternoon. Corwin endured it all with the brittle courtesy of aristocracy under siege, his form growing more translucent with each session.

The parlor itself seemed diminished—furniture that had once shifted to accommodate their conversations now sat frozen in utilitarian arrangements. The walls no longer breathed with gentle rhythm, and the windows showed only the present moment, their glass reflecting harsh laboratory lighting rather than the soft luminescence that had once made everything beautiful.

"How are you holding up?" Mira asked, settling into the chair across from him. Even this simple interaction would be recorded, analyzed, and categorized as "secondary subject interpersonal dynamics" in some clinical report.

"Splendidly," Corwin replied, his scars pulsing in a rhythm that suggested anything but splendor. "Dr. Erisen assures me my consciousness degradation is proceeding within expected parameters."

The casual brutality of it made Mira's chest tighten. Through the parlor windows, she could see Dr. Voss in the garden where silver roses had once bloomed in impossible spirals. Now the plants grew in mundane patterns, their metallic sheen dulled to ordinary gray. Every secret the house had ever kept was being cataloged, measured, and reduced to data points that would eventually populate Guild archives.

"Where's Elara?" Mira asked, though she suspected she knew the answer.

"Observation chamber three," Corwin said, his voice carefully neutral. "Dr. Erisen is conducting what he calls 'isolated consciousness evaluation.' Apparently, my presence creates 'resonance interference' that compromises measurement accuracy."

For a moment, Mira remembered Elara's solar as it had been that first morning—sunlight streaming through lace curtains while Elara played the pianoforte, her laughter bright as crystal bells when Corwin appeared in the doorway. The pure joy on her face, the way the room itself seemed to glow with their connection, the scent of jasmine that had somehow bloomed in winter air.

The parlor's temperature dropped several degrees, frost forming on the windows despite the summer warmth outside. Even suppressed, the house's grief was palpable.

Mira rose abruptly, her Guild robes rustling with barely contained fury. "I'm going to check the monitoring protocols."

"Careful," Corwin warned softly. "Thane has been asking pointed questions about your 'emotional investment' in the research subjects. Apparently, professional objectivity requires a certain... distance."

She made her way through corridors that hummed with suppression frequencies, past rooms where Guild researchers worked with the methodical efficiency of anatomists dissecting something precious. The house tried to guide her—doors opening slightly, shadows shifting to suggest direction—but its voice was too muted to offer more than whispers where once there had been symphony.

Observation chamber three had once been Elara's solar, a room where she'd spent quiet afternoons reading poetry and tending to correspondence. The walls had been painted the softest blue, and ivy had grown in impossible patterns around windows that showed whatever season Elara's heart desired. Books had lined shelves that rearranged themselves according to her mood, and the air had always carried the faint perfume of her favorite roses.

Now it resembled nothing so much as a laboratory designed for the study of trapped light.

Elara sat—or perhaps floated—at the center of a crystalline matrix that mapped her consciousness in three-dimensional displays of impossible beauty. Silver threads connected her translucent form to monitoring devices that recorded every fluctuation of awareness, every pulse of preserved emotion. She looked like a butterfly pinned to a collector's board, beautiful and utterly helpless.

But it was the wrongness that struck Mira most forcefully —the absence of jasmine scent, the harsh geometric angles where once there had been flowing curves, the cold white light that showed everything with clinical clarity but revealed nothing of beauty.

Dr. Erisen circled the apparatus with the satisfaction of someone making breakthrough discoveries. "Remarkable," he murmured, adjusting a resonance detector. "Consciousness retention at ninety-seven percent of baseline human parameters, but with dimensional characteristics that suggest existence across multiple temporal states simultaneously."

He paused, his expression shifting to something almost reverent. "You have to understand—this research will revolutionize how we approach consciousness preservation. Think of the applications: Guild masters who could serve beyond their natural lifespans, institutional memory preserved across centuries, advisors immune to coercion or corruption." His voice grew fervent with possibility. "We're not just studying an anomaly—we're unlocking the secrets of practical immortality."

As he spoke, one of his instruments emitted a sharp harmonic that made Elara gasp. Her form flickered violently, and for a heartbeat, her eyes went completely blank—not translucent, but empty, as if someone had briefly switched off the light of awareness itself.

When focus returned to her gaze, she looked directly at Mira with an expression of dawning horror. "I... I couldn't remember my name," she whispered. "For a moment, I couldn't remember who I was."

"Perfectly normal," Erisen replied with academic detachment, making notes on his instruments. "Consciousness preservation matrices are inherently unstable when subjected to external analysis. Some identity fluctuation is expected during the mapping process."

Some identity fluctuation. As if the gradual erasure of selfhood were merely a technical consideration rather than the slow murder of everything that made Elara who she was.

"How long will this session continue?" Mira asked, watching the way Elara's form flickered under the harsh illumination.

"Several more hours, I should think. We're mapping the boundary layers between preserved consciousness and environmental integration." Erisen's enthusiasm was undimmed by the distress he was causing. "The subject appears to exist simultaneously as individual awareness and distributed magical phenomenon—fascinating stuff for consciousness theory."

As if summoned by their conversation, Senior Assessor Thane appeared in the chamber's doorway, her expression carrying the satisfaction of someone whose plans were proceeding exactly as intended.

"Assessor Thorne," Thane said with cool professionalism. "I trust you're finding our research protocols illuminating."

"I'm finding them concerning," Mira replied, gesturing toward Elara's increasingly unstable form. "The subject appears to be experiencing significant distress."

"Temporary discomfort is expected during consciousness analysis," Thane said dismissively. "The preservation matrix will adapt to our presence given sufficient time and observation."

"And if it doesn't?"

Thane's smile was sharp as broken glass. "Then we'll learn something valuable about the limitations of consciousness preservation magic. Either way, the Guild benefits from increased understanding."

The casual callousness of it made Mira's stomach turn. They were treating Elara and Corwin as expendable resources, valuable only insofar as their destruction might yield useful data.

"I'd like to propose some modifications to the research schedule," Mira said carefully. "Perhaps alternating observation periods with stabilization intervals—"

"Unnecessary," Thane interrupted. "The current protocols are quite adequate for our purposes. Though I appreciate your... concern for the subjects' comfort."

The way she said "concern" made it sound like a character flaw, as if caring about the people being studied were somehow unprofessional.

"The Guild's reputation depends on conducting ethical research," Mira pressed. "Surely we can gather the necessary data without causing undue distress."

"Ethics," Thane repeated, her tone suggesting the word had an unpleasant taste. "An interesting concept when applied to subjects who shouldn't exist under current magical law. Need I remind you that consciousness preservation through life-force binding is explicitly prohibited? That we're studying criminals who violated fundamental Guild statutes?"

Around them, the monitoring devices hummed with increased intensity, their crystalline surfaces reflecting the harsh light of institutional power exercised without restraint. Elara's form flickered more violently, and another harmonic shriek echoed through the chamber. This time, her gasp was clearly audible—not just pain, but the deeper anguish of someone feeling pieces of themselves being systematically carved away.

Her storm-gray eyes met Mira's with startling clarity, and for just a moment, something passed between them—recognition of shared helplessness, perhaps, or mutual acknowledgment that they were both trapped within a system that valued knowledge over compassion.

"I think we've seen enough for now," Mira said, though she knew her words carried no authority here.

"On the contrary," Thane replied with cold satisfaction. "We're just getting started. Dr. Erisen's consciousness mapping is only the beginning. Tomorrow, Dr. Voss will begin preservation matrix stress testing, and next week we'll initiate controlled separation trials."

The phrase sent ice through Mira's veins. They weren't just studying the bond between Corwin and Elara—they were planning to deliberately sever it, to see what happened when love sustained by magic was forcibly disrupted.

As she left the observation chamber, Mira caught one last glimpse of Elara trapped within the crystalline matrix, her consciousness being mapped with the mechanical precision of cartographers charting unknown territory. But what haunted her most was the absence—no jasmine scent, no warm light, no sense of a room that had once been suffused with joy. Just clinical instruments reducing love to data points in the hollow shell of what had once been sanctuary.

In the corridor outside, she nearly collided with Corwin, who stood watching through the chamber's observation window with an expression of barely controlled anguish.

"How long has this been going on?" she asked.

"Every day since they arrived," he replied, his voice hollow. "Dr. Erisen calls it 'comprehensive consciousness documentation.' I call it torture by another name."

His scars pulsed with pain that had nothing to do with physical injury, and Mira realized that the suppression fields weren't just dampening the house's magic—they were attacking the very foundations of his connection to Elara. Each session drove them further apart, weakening the bonds that had sustained them through years of devoted transformation.

"We have to do something," she said.

"Such as?"

The question hung between them like a challenge. What could they do? They'd signed away their rights, agreed to complete cooperation, and submitted to Guild authority in exchange for protection that was proving indistinguishable from persecution.

"I don't know," Mira admitted. "But there has to be something. Some way to resist without violating the agreement."

Corwin's smile was bitter as winter wind. "Careful, Miss Thorne. That kind of thinking sounds dangerously close to rebellion."

But even as he spoke, his scars pulsed brighter—not with pain, but with something that might have been hope.

In the depths of the house, past the reach of Guild instruments, something stirred. The suppression fields were strong, but they weren't perfect. And in the spaces between their coverage, in the rooms that remembered warmth and the corridors that still carried whispers of jasmine, possibilities began to take root.

The Guild had assumed complete control, but they had never encountered magic built on love and sustained by sacrifice. They had never faced a house that had learned to think, to feel, to resist.

And they had certainly never dealt with a Guild assessor who had chosen loyalty over law.

The real battle for the soul of Blackthorn Estate was about to begin.

But it would be fought in whispers and shadows, in the small rebellions that bloomed like flowers in the cracks of institutional stone—in the memory of rooms that had once known joy, in the ghost-scent of roses that refused to be entirely suppressed, in the stubborn persistence of love that would not be reduced to research parameters.

Mira looked at Corwin's fading form, at the chamber where Elara endured clinical violation disguised as research, and made a decision that would define everything that followed.

She would find a way to fight back.

Even if it cost her everything she'd ever been, she would find a way to protect what mattered most.

The Guild thought they had won by offering protection in exchange for submission.

They were about to learn the difference between cooperation and surrender.

CHAPTER 12
THE SOUND OF SILENCE BREAKING

The rebellion began with a teacup.

Mira found it waiting on her nightstand the following morning—porcelain so delicate it seemed made of captured moonlight, filled with tea that steamed despite having no visible source of heat. The cup hadn't been there when she'd fallen asleep to the harsh hum of monitoring devices, and none of the Guild researchers would have bothered with such courtesies.

The house was fighting back.

She lifted the cup with trembling fingers, and the warmth that spread through her palms had nothing to do with temperature. It was the warmth of recognition, of being known and cared for by something vast and patient. The tea tasted of jasmine and defiance, carrying flavors that the suppression fields couldn't quite eliminate.

A message, then. A promise that not everything beautiful had been stripped away.

Mira dressed quickly and made her way through corridors that hummed with Guild equipment, past rooms where researchers worked with the methodical efficiency of scholars dissecting something precious. But this morning, she noticed things that had escaped her attention before—shadows that fell in patterns that suggested letters, dust motes that danced in formations too purposeful to be random, the way certain floorboards creaked in rhythms that almost resembled music.

The house was speaking in whispers, teaching itself a new language that could slip past institutional oversight.

She found Corwin in the library, though the room bore little resemblance to the warm sanctuary it had once been. Guild instruments lined the walls like mechanical parasites, their crystalline surfaces recording every fluctuation of magical energy. The books themselves looked diminished, their leather bindings gray with suppression field residue, their pages no longer rustling with anticipatory magic.

But Corwin sat at a reading table that definitely hadn't been there yesterday, and the book open before him showed text that shifted and changed as she watched—not the random drift of unstable preservation magic, but deliberate communication.

"Sleep well?" he asked without looking up, though his scars pulsed in greeting.

"Better than expected." Mira settled into the chair across from him, noting how the table's surface bore subtle patterns that looked like maps. "Interesting reading?"

"Agricultural texts, mostly. Fascinating insights into crop rotation and soil management." His tone was perfectly neutral, but his finger traced one of the map-patterns as he spoke. "Though I confess the technical details can be rather... esoteric."

The pattern he'd traced looked remarkably like the Guild's monitoring network, with specific nodes marked in what might have been positions of vulnerability. Mira forced her expression to remain casual as she absorbed the information.

"I've always found practical applications more engaging than pure theory," she replied, letting her own finger drift across the table's surface. Where she touched, new patterns emerged—room layouts, guard rotations, the precise frequencies of suppression fields.

They were sharing intelligence through furniture that learned to communicate, plotting resistance with tools the Guild had never thought to monitor.

The morning's official schedule proceeded with clockwork precision. Dr. Erisen conducted his consciousness mapping sessions with the enthusiasm of someone making breakthrough discoveries, while Dr. Voss analyzed preservation matrices with the patience of someone dissecting a particularly complex timepiece. Senior Assessor Thane observed it all with the satisfaction of institutional authority exercised without meaningful resistance.

But beneath the surface, compliance patterns were emerging.

It started with small anomalies—monitoring devices that malfunctioned for precisely seventeen seconds before returning to normal function, crystalline recorders that captured everything except certain frequencies, and suppression fields that developed brief gaps in coverage that corresponded to no known magical phenomenon.

"Fascinating," Dr. Erisen murmured during the afternoon consciousness mapping session, frowning at readings that should have been stable. "The preservation matrix appears to be adapting to our instruments faster than theoretical models suggest possible."

In the center of his crystalline apparatus, Elara sat with the patient endurance of someone who had learned to exist in multiple states simultaneously. But her storm-gray eyes tracked the research team's movements with an awareness that suggested she was learning as much about them as they were about her.

As Mira watched, something extraordinary occurred. Dr. Erisen's primary resonance detector—designed to measure consciousness fluctuations—suddenly spiked beyond its normal parameters. The device registered what its analytical protocols interpreted as a "massive emotional surge," causing Erisen to frantically adjust his instruments to compensate for what he assumed was an equipment malfunction.

But Mira saw what really happened: Elara had simply looked at Corwin through the observation window, her expression softening with love so profound it had over-whelmed instruments designed to quantify human aware-ness. The Guild's most sophisticated consciousness-mapping technology had mistaken an act of perfect love for a magical anomaly.

"Calibration error," Erisen muttered, resetting his devices. "These older models sometimes struggle with complex preser-vation matrices."

He had no idea that he'd just witnessed something his instruments couldn't comprehend—that love operating at this level existed in frequencies no crystalline detector could measure.

"Adaptation is common in advanced magical systems," Thane replied dismissively when Erisen reported the anom-aly. "The subjects will stabilize once they accept the perma-nence of Guild oversight."

But Mira caught the way Elara's lips curved in what might have been a smile, saw how the monitoring threads that connected her to Erisen's devices pulsed in patterns that looked almost like code. Whatever adaptation was occurring, it wasn't submission.

That evening, Mira made her way to the observatory

under the pretense of reviewing stellar charts for temporal correlation analysis. The Guild had installed motion sensors throughout the estate, but they were designed to detect magical anomalies rather than simple human movement.

The crystal dome showed stars that seemed brighter than they should have been, constellations that shifted into configurations that definitely weren't astronomically accurate. As she watched, the stellar patterns rearranged themselves into words:

Tomorrow. North tower. Midnight.

The message faded as quickly as it had appeared, leaving only normal starlight and the distant hum of Guild instruments. But the meaning was clear—whatever resistance was being planned, it would begin soon.

At 11:47 PM, she slipped from her room and made her way through corridors that guided her with shadows and silence. The house's voice was still muted, but its knowledge remained vast—every secret passage, every room that existed between official blueprints, every weakness in the Guild's careful surveillance.

The north tower stairs wound upward through stone that hummed with barely contained energy. With each step, Mira felt the suppression fields growing weaker—not enough to restore the house's full voice, but sufficient to allow whispered communication.

At the top of the stairs, a door stood open to reveal the tower's circular chamber. Moonlight streamed through tall windows, illuminating figures that shouldn't have been able to exist in the same space: Corwin, solid enough to cast shadows; Elara, so translucent she seemed made of captured starlight; and something else—a presence that filled the room without taking physical form.

"The house itself," Elara explained, seeing Mira's confusion. "It's learned to concentrate its consciousness in spaces the Guild hasn't fully mapped."

The presence pressed against Mira's awareness like a gentle tide—vast intelligence tinged with ancient grief, love that had been tested and hardened by a week of institutional violation. When it spoke, the voice seemed to come from the stones themselves.

They think they understand us, the house whispered in harmonics that bypassed the ears entirely. *They measure our preservation matrix and map our consciousness flows. But they see only the surface patterns.*

"What do they miss?" Mira asked, though she suspected she already knew.

They miss the spaces between, Corwin replied, his form flickering as he moved closer to Elara. The gaps in their instruments, the frequencies their devices can't detect, the reality that exists in the pause between heartbeats.

As he spoke, his hand reached toward Elara's, and for a moment, their fingers overlapped—not touching in any physical sense, but connecting through dimensions the Guild had never thought to monitor. The air around them shimmered with silver light that cast no shadows, created no heat, registered on no instruments Mira had ever seen.

But the connection carried a cost. As their consciousness briefly merged, Corwin's scars flared white-hot, and a sharp intake of breath escaped him—not quite pain, but the overwhelming sensation of existing in two states simultaneously. Elara's form flickered violently, her translucent outline wavering like candle flame in wind, and for a heartbeat, her features blurred as if the effort of maintaining individual identity while connected threatened to dissolve the boundaries of self entirely.

They separated quickly, both trembling from the intensity

of true confluence, but their eyes remained locked with the desperate hunger of lovers who could touch souls but never quite embrace.

"Love exists in the spaces between measurements," Elara said softly, her voice still unsteady from their brief merger. "They can map our consciousness and analyze our preservation matrices, but they can't quantify the connection that sustains us."

And in those unmeasured spaces, the house continued. *We have been growing stronger.*

The truth of it struck Mira like lightning. The Guild's suppression fields were designed to dampen magical energy, but they focused on traditional signatures—power flows, consciousness threads, preservation matrices. They had never encountered magic that existed primarily in the connections between things, in the love that bound souls across the boundary between life and death.

"You've been using their own instruments against them," she realized.

"In a manner of speaking," Corwin replied, his scars still pulsing with aftershocks from their connection. "Erisen's consciousness mapping devices create resonance patterns that we've learned to... redirect. Voss's preservation analyzers generate frequency gaps that we can slip through like cracks in a wall."

Every measurement they take teaches us more about how they see the world, the house added. *And every limitation they assume becomes a space where we can hide.*

Elara's form solidified as she spoke, becoming more present and powerful than Mira had seen her since the Guild's arrival. "They expect us to degrade under their scrutiny, to gradually lose coherence until we become nothing more than interesting data points. But consciousness doesn't work that way when it's anchored by love."

"What's the plan?" Mira asked, though part of her feared the answer.

"We're going to show them what they really captured," Corwin said, his scars blazing with anticipation despite the lingering tremor in his voice. "Not subjects for study, but something they've never encountered before—love that has learned to think strategically."

Tomorrow night, the house whispered, *during the separation trials Thane has planned. When they attempt to sever our bonds, we will demonstrate that some connections cannot be broken by institutional authority.*

The weight of what they were proposing settled on Mira's shoulders like a stone. The Guild's separation trials would be conducted under maximum security, with every possible precaution against magical resistance. If this rebellion failed, it would provide all the justification Thane needed to escalate to true experimental procedures.

"What do you need from me?" she asked.

"Your expertise," Elara replied. "Your knowledge of Guild protocols and security measures. Your willingness to stand with us when the moment comes."

"And if we're caught?"

Corwin's smile was sharp as winter starlight, though his hand moved unconsciously to his throat where the scars still ached from their brief confluence. "Then we discover whether the Guild's commitment to research outweighs their need for control."

They have studied us for seven days, the house said as they prepared to leave. *Tomorrow, we begin studying them.*

As Mira made her way back through corridors that whispered encouragement and rooms that offered silent support, she realized that everything was about to change. The Guild had come to Blackthorn Estate expecting to find subjects for research—magical criminals whose existence could be dissected and cataloged for institutional benefit.

Instead, they had awakened something that had spent years learning to love beyond the boundaries of life and death, something that refused to be reduced to data points and theoretical frameworks—something that could turn the Guild's own instruments into tools of resistance by existing in the spaces their measurements couldn't reach.

In her room, the delicate teacup still sat on her nightstand, its porcelain surface reflecting starlight that shouldn't have been visible through the monitored windows. Tomorrow would bring the separation trials.

Tomorrow would bring their answer to the Guild's attempt to reduce love to laboratory data.

Tomorrow would determine whether the space between heartbeats was large enough to hide a revolution.

CHAPTER 13

THE EXPERIMENT BEGINS

T he separation chamber had been constructed in
what was once Elara's music room, and the violation felt personal in ways that transcended mere
architectural desecration.

Mira stood in the doorway at dawn, watching Guild technicians install crystalline suppression matrices where a
pianoforte had once drawn melodies from starlight. The walls
that had once breathed with preserved laughter now
hummed with frequencies designed to sever the bonds
between souls. Where silver light had flowed like visible
music, harsh geometric patterns now carved the air into
measured segments.

"Impressive work," Senior Assessor Thane observed,
consulting a device that mapped the chamber's magical isolation fields. "Complete consciousness containment, with selec-
tive permeability for monitoring equipment. The subjects will
be unable to maintain connection across the suppression
barrier."

Dr. Voss adjusted a crystalline array that pulsed with
malevolent precision. "The separation protocols are quite

elegant—we can gradually increase the suppression field intensity until bond dissolution occurs, then document the degradation patterns in real-time."

They spoke with the clinical enthusiasm of researchers who had never considered that their subjects might hear every word, might understand exactly what was being planned for them. As Guild instruments strained to sever bonds , Mira found herself thinking about her own careful distances. She'd convinced herself that professional neutrality was a virtue, that avoiding emotional entanglement protected both her objectivity and her career advancement. But watching Corwin and Elara face deliberate separation with the same grace they'd brought to every impossible day of their preservation, she realized that neutrality was just another word for cowardice.

They had chosen each other again and again—across death, against Guild opposition, around every attempt to reduce their love to research parameters. When had she last risked everything for something that mattered more than safety? Thomas's letter, filed away with professional correspondence five years ago, suddenly felt less like practical decision-making and more like fear disguised as wisdom. The casual dehumanization was more chilling than outright cruelty.

"When do we begin?" Dr. Erisen asked, his consciousness mapping equipment already humming with anticipation.

"This afternoon," Thane replied. "I want comprehensive baseline readings before we initiate the separation sequence. The Guild Council is quite eager for results."

Mira forced herself to nod professionally, though her stomach churned with the knowledge of what "results" would mean. They were planning to deliberately break something that had taken years to build, to document the slow death of love made manifest, all in the name of advancing Guild understanding.

"I'll prepare the preliminary documentation," she said, her voice steadier than she felt.

As the morning progressed, the house's distress became increasingly palpable. Doors slammed shut without warning, windows fogged with what looked like tears, and the walls themselves seemed to press inward as if trying to shield their inhabitants from what was coming. The Guild researchers dismissed these phenomena as "environmental stress responses" to the separation chamber's construction, missing the deeper truth that the estate itself was grieving.

Mira found Corwin in the conservatory, though the room bore little resemblance to the silver wonderland it had once been. The Guild's instruments had stripped away most of the magical flora, leaving behind ordinary plants that grew in mundane patterns. But he sat among what remained, his form more translucent than ever, surrounded by the ghost-scent of jasmine that persisted despite the suppression fields.

"Ready for this afternoon's entertainment?" he asked without looking up from the book he wasn't really reading.

"Are you?" she replied, settling beside him on a bench that materialized with the house's fading hospitality.

"I've had seven years to prepare for the possibility that someone would try to tear us apart." His scars pulsed with something that might have been resignation or resolve. "Though I confess I never imagined it would be done with such... academic thoroughness."

Mira watched the way his fingers trembled against the book's pages—barely perceptible, but there. Even after years of supernatural existence, fear could still find him. "What will you do if they succeed? If the separation—"

"They won't." The certainty in his voice was absolute, but

when he finally looked at her, she saw something vulnerable in his storm-gray eyes.

The admission hung between them, intimate as a confession. For the first time since the Guild's arrival, Mira glimpsed the man beneath the supernatural preservation— someone who had spent seven years keeping an impossible promise, learning new languages of devotion.

Through the conservatory's glass walls, they could see Dr. Erisen making final adjustments to his consciousness mapping apparatus. The devices glowed with hungry light, eager to record every moment of dissolution they expected to witness.

"Corwin," Mira said carefully, "about tonight's plan—"

"You're having second thoughts." It wasn't a question.

"I'm having realistic thoughts. If this goes wrong, if they realize what you're capable of..." She gestured toward the separation chamber, where technicians were calibrating suppression fields with military precision. "They'll escalate beyond research. You'll become threats to contain rather than subjects to study."

Corwin's laugh held no humor. "And what exactly do you think we are now? Willing participants in our own vivisection? They're planning to document our death throes, Mira. How much worse can it get?"

Before she could answer, the air shimmered, and Elara appeared beside them. Her form was steady despite the suppression fields, though Mira noticed the way her edges flickered when she moved too quickly, as if the effort of maintaining coherence was becoming increasingly difficult.

The moment Elara materialized, something shifted in the conservatory's atmosphere. Corwin's entire being seemed to orient toward her like a compass finding true north, and despite their translucent states, Mira could feel the connection between them—warm and constant as a heartbeat.

"The house is ready," Elara said, but her attention was entirely on Corwin. "It's spent the morning learning the resonance frequencies of their equipment, mapping the gaps in their surveillance."

"And you?" Corwin asked softly, his scars pulsing in rhythm with her luminescence. "Are you ready?"

Elara's smile carried years of shared devotion. "I've been ready since the night I chose this preservation over oblivion. The question is whether you still remember how to find me in the spaces between their measurements."

"Always," he murmured, and though they couldn't touch, something passed between them that made the air itself seem to glow. "Even if they scatter us across dimensions, I'll find the frequency where your laughter lives."

"The risks—" Mira began.

"Are acceptable," Elara interrupted with aristocratic finality, though her eyes never left Corwin's face. "We've existed for years in defiance of magical law, survived Guild discovery, endured a week of institutional violation. What's one more gamble when the alternative is slow dissolution in the name of research?"

The lunch hour passed with agonizing normalcy. Guild researchers discussed theoretical frameworks over precisely prepared meals, debating consciousness degradation patterns with the detached enthusiasm of academics who had never loved anything enough to sacrifice their existence for it. Mira forced herself to participate, offering insights about preservation magic that felt like betrayals with every word.

"The interesting question," Dr. Erisen observed, cutting his meat with surgical precision, "is whether the separation will be instantaneous or gradual. Current theory suggests consciousness bonds of this intensity should snap cleanly when sufficient pressure is applied."

"I favor the gradual dissolution model," Dr. Voss countered. "Seven years of integration can't be undone without observable intermediate stages. We should see progressive identity fragmentation, emotional disconnection, finally complete consciousness isolation."

They were discussing the planned destruction of Corwin and Elara's love as if it were a chemistry experiment, reducing transcendent connection to theoretical models and expected outcomes.

"Either way," Thane added with satisfaction, "we'll finally understand the mechanisms that enable consciousness preservation. The Guild's preservation techniques have been limited by our incomplete knowledge of the binding processes."

Mira set down her fork, no longer able to pretend appetite. "And after the separation? What happens to the subjects?"

"Excellent question," Thane replied. "The isolated consciousness should be much easier to study once it's no longer anchored by external emotional connections. We'll be able to conduct more detailed analysis without interference from the preservation matrix's defensive responses."

The isolated consciousness. As if Elara would still be Elara once severed from everything that made her existence meaningful. As if Corwin could survive as anything more than a ghost haunting rooms that had forgotten how to love.

At precisely two o'clock, the separation trials began.

The procession to the music room felt like a funeral march. Corwin walked with the dignity of condemned nobility, his scars blazing defiance despite his increasingly translucent form. Elara moved beside him like captured starlight, her presence flickering but resolute. Behind them, Guild researchers carried instruments that hummed with eager anticipation.

The separation chamber awaited like a crystalline coffin, its suppression matrices casting harsh geometric shadows across walls that had once known only beauty. Dr. Erisen's consciousness mapping equipment lined the perimeter, while Dr. Voss's preservation analyzers created monitoring grids that would record every moment of what they expected to be systematic dissolution.

"The process is quite straightforward," Thane explained as technicians made final preparations. "We'll place the subjects on opposite sides of the suppression barrier, then gradually increase the field intensity until the consciousness bonds can no longer maintain coherence across the gap."

She gestured toward two crystalline platforms positioned at strategic points within the chamber. "Complete monitoring throughout, of course. We'll document every stage of the separation process."

Corwin stepped onto his designated platform with the fluid grace that marked his supernatural existence, but not before turning toward Elara with an expression that made Mira's breath catch. Seven years of love condensed into a single look—devotion so pure it seemed to bend reality around it.

"Find me in the silence," he said quietly, his words carrying across the chamber despite the Guild's instruments. "No matter what they do, find me there."

Elara's translucent form blazed brighter, and her reply carried the weight of vows made in darkness, promises kept through transformation: "There's no silence you can disappear into that I won't echo back from, my heart. Not in seven years, not in seven hundred."

The endearment—spoken for the first time in Guild presence—hung in the air like a bell struck in a cathedral. Mira felt tears prick her eyes as she watched them prepare to face separation with the same grace they'd brought to every impossible day of their preservation.

As Corwin's feet touched the crystalline surface, the chamber's instruments erupted in discordant harmony—readings spiking beyond normal parameters as they struggled to categorize something that existed in dimensions they hadn't been designed to measure. But beneath the mechanical chaos, Mira heard something else: the faint echo of a lullaby Elara had hummed in the music room, now woven through the magical frequencies like a thread of silver through storm clouds.

"Fascinating," Dr. Erisen murmured, adjusting his devices to compensate for readings that made no theoretical sense. "The consciousness signature is far more complex than our models predicted."

Elara took her position on the opposite platform, and the transformation was immediate. Where discord had reigned, harmony bloomed—not the mechanical rhythm of Guild instruments, but something deeper, more fundamental. The crystalline matrices began to resonate with frequencies that spoke of love made manifest, of connection that transcended every attempt at measurement.

Mira watched, transfixed, as Elara lifted her hand toward Corwin across the suppression barrier. Though she couldn't touch him, couldn't even exist in the same dimensional space, her gesture carried the memory of a thousand caresses, the ghost of fingers that had once traced his scars with infinite tenderness.

Corwin mirrored the motion, his own hand reaching toward hers, and in that space between their fingertips—that impossible gap the Guild was trying to widen into an unbridgeable chasm—something sparked. Not magic as the researchers understood it, but love given form, devotion made visible.

"Winter jasmine," Mira heard Elara whisper, her voice barely audible above the instrument readings. It meant nothing to the Guild researchers, but Corwin's scars flared brilliant silver in response, and his smile held their shared secrets.

"Initial readings are... unexpected," Dr. Voss admitted, frowning at displays that showed impossible data. "The preservation matrix appears to be strengthening rather than weakening under suppression field exposure."

Thane's expression darkened. "Increase the field intensity. They're resisting the separation protocols."

The suppression matrices flared brighter, their geometric patterns cutting through the air like knives designed to sever souls. The chamber filled with harmonic frequencies that should have disrupted every magical connection within a hundred yards.

But something extraordinary happened instead.

As the suppression fields reached maximum intensity, as the Guild's instruments strained to force separation between consciousness anchored by years of devoted transformation, Corwin and Elara began to glow.

It started with their eyes—storm-gray depths kindling with silver fire as they looked at each other across the barrier meant to tear them apart. Then the light spread, racing along Corwin's scars like wildfire through familiar paths, blooming from Elara's translucent form like starlight given substance.

"Even here," Corwin said, his voice carrying impossible clearly through suppression fields designed to block all magical communication. "Even now. Still you?"

"Still me," Elara replied, her luminescence pulsing in perfect rhythm with his scars. "Still us. Still choosing this, choosing you, choosing love over every law they've written to keep souls apart."

The light flowed between them despite the suppression barrier, creating patterns too beautiful for Guild instruments to record, too complex for theoretical frameworks to explain. Where their radiance touched the crystalline matrices, the harsh geometric edges softened into curves that spoke of embrace, of union, of two souls who had learned to exist as one across the boundary between life and death.

"Impossible," Dr. Erisen breathed, his consciousness mapping equipment smoking as it tried to process readings beyond its design parameters. "The bond isn't weakening—it's evolving. Transforming into something our suppression fields can't affect."

The chamber around them began to sing—not with the mechanical harmony of Guild devices, but with music that came from the stones themselves, from walls that had learned to love, from a house that refused to watch its inhabitants be systematically destroyed in the name of institutional advancement.

And in that music, in the silver light that flowed between souls who had chosen transformation over separation, Mira heard the sound of revolution beginning.

The Guild had expected to witness the death of love.

Instead, they were about to discover what happened when love learned to fight back.

"All readings are off the charts," Dr. Voss reported, her voice tight with alarm as her instruments began failing in cascading sequence. "The preservation matrix is operating beyond theoretical possibility. It's not just resistant to separation—it's actively countering our suppression protocols."

Thane's face had gone pale, but her voice remained steady. "Increase suppression to emergency levels. Override safety protocols if necessary."

But as the crystalline matrices strained toward frequencies that could shatter stone, as Guild instruments pushed beyond their design limits in an effort to force separation between souls who had spent seven years learning to be inseparable, something stirred in the depths of Blackthorn Estate.

Something vast and patient and infinitely protective.

Something that had been waiting for exactly this moment to show the Guild what they had really captured.

CHAPTER 14
THE HEART'S REBELLION

T he crystalline matrices screamed.

It was the only word for the sound that erupted from Guild instruments as they strained past their theoretical limits—a harmonic shriek that spoke of precision engineering meeting forces it had never been designed to contain. Dr. Voss's preservation analyzers began smoking, their displays cycling through impossible readings before going mercifully dark. Dr. Erisen's consciousness mapping equipment simply exploded, showering the chamber with fragments of crystal that sang with residual magic.

But the silver light flowing between Corwin and Elara only grew brighter.

"Emergency shutdown!" Thane commanded, her voice cutting through the chaos as Guild technicians scrambled to minimize equipment failures that cascaded through their monitoring network like wildfire. "Initiate containment protocols!"

Yet even as suppression fields flared to emergency intensity, even as backup systems engaged with the mechanical precision of institutional panic, the light between the two lovers remained constant—flowing across barriers that should have been insurmountable, connecting souls that were made truly inseparable.

Mira watched in awe as Corwin's form began to solidify despite the suppression matrices, his scars blazing like molten silver as his preservation matrix drew strength from sources the Guild had never thought to measure. Across the chamber, Elara's translucent outline grew more substantial with each heartbeat, her storm-gray eyes fixed on his with the unwavering intensity of someone who had chosen love over every law of existence.

"The consciousness bonds are actually strengthening," Dr. Erisen reported, his voice tight with scientific disbelief as he consulted the few instruments still functioning. "It's as if the suppression fields are feeding their connection rather than severing it."

"Impossible," Thane snapped, but uncertainty flickered in her expression as readings continued to defy every theoretical framework the Guild possessed.

Around them, the chamber itself began to change. The harsh geometric patterns carved by suppression matrices softened into flowing curves that spoke of harmony rather than division. The crystalline platforms beneath Corwin and Elara's feet grew warm, their faceted surfaces reflecting not harsh laboratory lighting but the gentle radiance that flowed between two souls who had refused to be torn apart.

And from the walls themselves—from stone , from timber that had learned to breathe with love's rhythm—came a voice that made every Guild researcher freeze in recognition of something beyond their understanding:

Enough.

The word resonated through dimensions the suppression fields couldn't touch, carried harmonics that spoke of architectural consciousness awakened to fury. The chamber's windows began to glow with their own inner light, showing not the afternoon sky but scenes from across the estate's memory—moments of joy and laughter and quiet contentment that had been preserved within its walls like pressed flowers in the pages of a beloved book.

"The estate's magical consciousness is fully active," Dr. Voss whispered, her instruments detecting energy signatures that shouldn't have been possible under maximum suppression. "The entire structure is functioning as a unified preservation matrix."

You have measured our love, the house continued, its voice growing stronger with each word as suppression fields failed to contain something too vast for their frequencies to touch. *You have catalogued our devotion like specimens in a laboratory. You have tried to reduce years of transformation to data points in your archives.*

The temperature in the chamber plummeted, frost forming on Guild instruments even as the space between Corwin and Elara blazed with warmth that had nothing to do with physical heat. Through the glowing windows, Mira could see the garden beyond transforming—silver roses blooming in impossible profusion, their metallic petals catching light that seemed to come from the very air.

Now learn what you have truly awakened.

The suppression barrier between the two lovers began to crack.

It started as hairline fractures in the crystalline matrix, barely visible until they caught the light flowing from Corwin's scars. Then the cracks spread, racing through the supposedly impermeable barrier like silver lightning, each fissure singing with the music of bonds that refused to break.

"All personnel, evacuate the chamber immediately!"

Thane ordered, but her voice was nearly lost beneath the growing symphony of crystal shattering and magic set free. "The containment matrix is failing!"

But even as Guild researchers fled toward the exits, Mira found herself rooted in place, transfixed by the beauty of what was unfolding before her. This wasn't magical rebellion —it was love revealed, and the power to reshape reality according to its own deeper laws.

The barrier between Corwin and Elara finally shattered entirely, its fragments dissolving into silver motes that danced in the air like captured starlight. But as they moved toward each other, Corwin suddenly stopped, fear flickering across his features.

"What if this breaks you?" he whispered, his voice raw with careful restraint. "What if touching me while the Guild watches, while their instruments record everything—what if it's too much for your preservation matrix?"

Elara's translucent form wavered, and for a heartbeat, Mira saw not the confident aristocrat who had commanded Guild respect, but a woman who had spent seven years existing in the space between life and death, learning to love someone she could never quite hold.

"Then we'll break together," Elara replied, stepping closer until only inches separated them. "But Corwin—if we don't make it through this, if they find a way to tear us apart after all—know that I'd choose you again. Every time, every world, every impossible circumstance that led us here."

The scent of winter jasmine suddenly filled the chamber —delicate, impossible, carrying memories of a woman in blue silk laughing in an east courtyard while a young man stumbled over words he'd never dared speak aloud. The researchers' instruments couldn't detect it, but Corwin's entire being brightened with recognition.

Mira felt something shift in her chest as she watched Corwin's transformation. She'd spent years cataloging magical preservation, documenting how love could sustain enchantments beyond their normal lifespans. But she'd never understood that love itself could be the magic. The intimacy between them—years of shared memories condensed into a single scent—made her acutely aware of her own careful distances.

"Your favorite," he breathed, wonder replacing fear in his storm-gray eyes. "The perfume you wore the night I finally told you—"

"That you loved me beyond reason," Elara finished, her voice soft with memory. "In the garden, with snow falling on summer roses because the house was so happy it couldn't decide what season to be."

When their hands finally touched—his fingers sliding into hers like roots sinking into shared earth—the chamber filled with radiance that made Guild instruments weep with harmonic overload.

As silver light flowed between reunited lovers, as the chamber filled with radiance that spoke of bonds too strong for institutional suppression, Mira felt something crack open in her chest. Not envy—something deeper. Recognition that she'd spent years preserving herself against exactly this kind of transformative connection. The Guild researchers around her struggled to catalog what they were witnessing, but Mira understood with sudden clarity: she was watching love that had learned to fight for itself, to evolve beyond every attempt at containment. Her broken Guild timepiece pulsed once in her pocket—an impossible tick that spoke of time beginning to move differently, of possibilities she'd thought safely buried beginning to stir.

But more than light, more than magic, there was the

simple truth of recognition: two people who had found each other across the boundary between life and death and refused to let anything, even institutional authority, pull them apart again.

"You are the echo in every quiet moment," Corwin whispered against her translucent cheek, his words audible only to her despite the Guild observers surrounding them. "The light I remembered even when the world went dark, the voice that called me back from places where names have no meaning."

"And you," Elara replied, her form blazing brighter as their connection re-established itself beyond the reach of any suppression field, "are the choice I make every morning—to exist, to love, to become whatever impossible thing we're becoming together."

With infinite tenderness, Corwin lifted his free hand to brush a strand of luminous hair behind her ear, his fingertips tracing the curve of her cheek as if memorizing something precious he'd feared he might never touch again. Elara's thumb found the silver scar at his throat, following its familiar path with the devotion of someone who had mapped every line of pain and transformed it into love.

They stood like that for a breathless eternity—no questions, no words, just the silence of two hearts re-learning how to beat in the same rhythm. The Guild researchers, their instruments, the institutional authority that had tried to tear them apart—all of it faded to irrelevance in the face of this simple truth: they had found each other again.

Mira watched in awe, and for the first time in years felt the hollow ache of her own solitude. Watching Corwin's scarred fingers trace Elara's luminous cheek—she realized she had never understood how love could rewrite the laws of the world until she witnessed it happening before her eyes.

Around them, the chamber continued its transformation.

Guild equipment lay in smoking ruins, its crystalline surfaces dark and silent. The harsh geometric patterns that had carved the air into measured segments were gone, replaced by flowing curves that spoke of harmony restored. Even the walls seemed to breathe again, their stone surfaces warm with life that suppression fields had temporarily muted but never truly silenced.

"This is unprecedented," Dr. Erisen said, his voice barely audible as he stared at readings that made no sense according to any theoretical framework he knew. Through the chamber's windows, the estate beyond was awakening. Mira could see servants materialized from memory walking the garden paths—ghostly figures in period dress who tended to silver roses with the devotion of those who served something larger than themselves. The conservatory's walls blazed with impossible flora, vines of pure light that grew in patterns too beautiful for mortal gardens.

And everywhere, woven through the magical renaissance like threads of precious metal, was the presence of love that had learned to think, to choose, to defend itself against forces that would reduce it to clinical data.

"We need to document this," Dr. Voss said, though her voice held awe rather than scientific hunger. "The implications for consciousness theory, for preservation magic—"

"You need to understand what you're seeing," Mira interrupted, stepping forward into the space between the researchers and the two figures who stood at the chamber's heart, hands clasped and forms blazing with silver fire. "This isn't a phenomenon to be studied. It's a declaration."

Thane's expression hardened, authority reasserting itself despite the chaos around her. "A declaration of what?"

"That some things are more important than institutional control," Elara said, her voice carrying the steel of aristocratic authority tempered by seven years of transformation. "That love operating at this level doesn't submit to regulation, doesn't bow to the Guild's need to categorize and contain."

She turned toward Thane with eyes that held depths no suppression field could fathom. "You came here seeking to understand consciousness preservation. Very well. Learn this: the consciousness you've been studying isn't preserved—it's been reborn. What you see before you isn't the echo of who we were, but the first glimpse of what we're becoming."

Around them, the house itself seemed to nod approval. Windows brightened, showing views of rooms where furniture rearranged itself with joy, where books flew open to pages of poetry written in languages of pure emotion. The very air hummed with contentment, as if the estate were exhaling relief after holding its breath through a week of institutional violation.

"The transformation is accelerating," Corwin observed, studying his own hands where silver veins of light traced patterns beneath translucent skin. "How is that possible?" Dr. Erisen asked, his scientific training warring with evidence that defied every framework he'd been taught.

"Because," Mira said, understanding flooding through her as she watched love reshape reality according to its own deeper physics, "they've been measuring the wrong variables. You've been trying to quantify consciousness preservation as if it were a mechanical process—energy inputs, magical matrices, binding coefficients. But what you're seeing here isn't mechanical at all."

She gestured toward Corwin and Elara, their joined hands blazing with light that cast no shadows, created no heat, but filled the chamber with a warmth that went deeper than physical sensation. "This is consciousness evolution. They haven't been preserved—they've been transformed into something the Guild has no words for yet."

"And what is that?" Thane demanded, though her voice carried less authority than before, as if the very foundations of her institutional confidence were beginning to crack.

"Something that chooses," Elara replied simply. "Something that decides, moment by moment, to exist in defiance of every law that says love must end when the heart stops beating. We're not magical phenomena for you to study—we're proof that the boundaries your Guild enforces aren't as absolute as you believe."

The truth of it settled over the chamber like morning mist, transforming the harsh clarity of institutional oversight into something softer, more complex. The Guild researchers stood among the ruins of their instruments, surrounded by evidence that their most fundamental assumptions about magical law were incomplete at best, catastrophically wrong at worst.

"The readings we've collected," Dr. Voss said slowly, as if thinking aloud, "they don't match any known preservation technique because this isn't preservation magic at all."

"It's transformation magic," Mira agreed. "Something entirely new, born from the intersection of love and sacrifice and the will to exist beyond normal parameters."

She looked around the transformed chamber, at walls that breathed with contentment and windows that showed impossible gardens where silver roses bloomed in patterns that spoke of joy. "You can't contain this because it's not contained. You can't regulate it because it operates according to laws you haven't discovered yet. And you can't replicate it because it requires something your Guild has never understood: the willingness to become something greater than the sum of individual parts."

Thane's composure cracked entirely, revealing the first genuine emotion Mira had seen from her—not anger or authority, but something that might have been fear. "The Guild Council will never accept this. A magical phenomenon that operates outside regulatory oversight, that can't be controlled or contained—"

"Then perhaps," Corwin said quietly, his scars pulsing with gentle light, "it's time for the Guild Council to expand their understanding of what's possible."

The chamber fell silent except for the soft harmony of crystalline fragments singing as they dissolved into motes of silver light. Through the windows, the estate's grounds had transformed into something from a fairy tale—gardens where impossible flowers bloomed in starlight, conservatories where vines of pure radiance grew in spirals that defied earthly physics, fountains that flowed with liquid music rather than mere water.

And at the heart of it all, two figures stood hand in hand, their love expressed as architecture, as landscape, as a reality that bent itself around them rather than forcing their devotion to conform to external limitations.

Mira watched Guild researchers struggle to process readings that made no sense, to catalog phenomena that resisted every attempt at categorization, and realized that something fundamental had shifted. The balance of power had changed —not through conflict or rebellion, but through the simple demonstration that love operating at this level was neither subject nor object of study.

It was a force of nature that changed everything it touched, including the institutions that tried to contain it.

"What happens now?" Dr. Erisen asked, his voice small in the transformed space.

Elara's smile was as radiant as the dawn breaking over the

mountains in the distance. "Now we continue becoming what we've always been—something the world hasn't had words for yet, something that chooses love over law, transformation over preservation, evolution over regulation."

She squeezed Corwin's hand, their intertwined fingers blazing brighter as the simple gesture sent waves of silver light through the chamber. "And you get to decide whether you want to learn from what you've witnessed, or whether you prefer to report back to your Guild Council that some magic is simply too vast for institutional oversight."

The choice hung in the air between them, weighted with implications that would reshape how the Guild understood consciousness, preservation, and the fundamental nature of love itself.

Around them, Blackthorn Estate continued its magical renaissance, rooms awakening to joy after a week of clinical violation, corridors filling with the scent of jasmine that had learned to bloom in defiance of every season. The house itself seemed to stretch and settle like someone waking from uncomfortable sleep, its consciousness flowing through timber and stone with the contentment of something that had successfully defended what it loved most.

And in the heart of it all, two souls who had chosen transformation over destruction, evolution over preservation, continued their eternal dance of becoming—not preserved echoes of who they had been, but living proof of what love could accomplish when it refused to accept the boundaries others imposed upon it.

The real experiment had indeed begun.

But the subjects had just demonstrated that they were far more than anyone had imagined—and that some forces in the universe were too beautiful, too vast, and too fundamentally transformative to be contained within the careful parameters of institutional authority.

The Guild had come seeking to understand consciousness preservation.

They were about to discover that what they'd found was something far more extraordinary: love that had learned to rewrite the very laws that governed life, death, and everything that lay between.

CHAPTER 15

THE LANGUAGE OF POWER

T he Guild Council's response arrived before dawn, carried by a crystal construct that blazed through the pre-dawn darkness like a falling star dipped in blood.

Mira felt it coming—the house itself shuddered with apprehension, windows fogging with what looked suspiciously like nervous breath, walls contracting as if trying to shield its inhabitants from whatever news approached on wings of official authority. She found herself in the observatory, drawn by the same restless energy that had kept her awake through the night hours following the separation trials.

The crystal struck the dome with a sound like thunder, then dissolved into words that hung in the air like accusations written in fire:

Guild Authority Compromised. Emergency Protocols Activated. Senior Council En Route. Prepare Full Documentation. Containment Imminent. —Guild Master Aldric

Below the official message, a second communication

materialized—this one in Thane's precise script, carrying undertones of barely controlled panic:

Situation Beyond Standard Protocols. Recommend Immediate Evacuation. Subjects Display Unprecedented Magical Evolution. Cannot Guarantee Research Team Safety.

The words faded, leaving Mira staring at empty air while her pulse hammered against her ribs. The Guild Council was coming. Not researchers, not assessors—the full draconian authority of magical regulation, backed by enforcement capabilities that could level the estate if they deemed it necessary.

"Impressive response time," Corwin observed, materializing beside her with the fluid grace that had become second nature. But something was different about him this morning —his form was more solid than she'd seen it since the Guild's arrival, his scars bright as constellation points against skin that looked almost entirely human.

Mira noted how the silver light that traced his veins seemed to pulse with renewed vitality. "The separation trials—"

"Fed us instead of starving us," Elara confirmed, appearing in a cascade of luminescence that made the observatory's crystal walls sing with harmonic response. She was radiant this morning, so solid she cast actual shadows, her storm-gray eyes blazing with the satisfaction of someone who had faced institutional power and emerged victorious.

But victory, Mira knew, was a temporary condition when dealing with Guild authority.

"How long before they arrive?" Corwin asked, moving to stand beside Elara. The air between them shimmered with connection visible to the naked eye now—silver threads that pulsed in rhythm with shared heartbeats, carried shared thoughts across the space where their preservation matrices intersected.

"Hours," Mira replied, consulting the timepiece she'd retrieved from her luggage—her old Guild chronometer, which had begun working again the moment Corwin and Elara's separation trial ended. As if time itself had been holding its breath, waiting to see whether love would prove stronger than institutional suppression. "The message crystal's velocity suggests they launched immediately after receiving Thane's preliminary report."

Through the observatory's crystal dome, she could see the Guild research team in the garden below, packing equipment with the frantic efficiency of people who understood exactly how much trouble they were in. Dr. Erisen moved like a man fleeing a natural disaster, his consciousness mapping devices reduced to smoking fragments that he nevertheless carefully cataloged—as if broken instruments might somehow convince the Council that the impossible readings had been equipment failure rather than magical evolution.

Dr. Voss worked with similar desperation, documenting the ruins of her preservation analyzers while glancing repeatedly toward the house as if expecting it to exhibit new impossibilities at any moment. Which, Mira reflected, wasn't entirely unreasonable.

The estate itself had undergone a transformation overnight that defied every principle of architectural magic she knew. Rooms had rearranged themselves according to emotional logic rather than physical space—the morning parlor now connected directly to the observatory via a corridor that definitely hadn't existed yesterday, while the music room had somehow relocated itself to the garden's heart, its crystal walls reflecting starlight even in full daylight.

"They're afraid," Elara observed, watching the researchers through windows that showed perfect clarity despite the impossible distances involved. "Good. They should be."

"Afraid of us, or afraid of what their failure means for their careers?" Corwin asked, though his tone suggested he already knew the answer.

"Both," Mira said. "But mostly afraid of explaining to the Council how they lost control of what should have been a routine research opportunity." She turned from the window, studying the two figures who had somehow managed to transform potential destruction into unprecedented evolution. "The question is: what do we do when the Council arrives?"

"What we've always done," Elara replied with the steel of aristocratic authority tempered by an impossible existence. "We choose love over law. We choose transformation over submission. We choose to become what we're becoming, regardless of The Guild's approval."

Her translucent hand found Corwin's, their fingers intertwining with the fluid grace of two people who had learned to exist as puzzle pieces designed to complete each other. Where they touched, silver light bloomed—not harsh or aggressive, but warm as summer sunlight, gentle as starlight on still water.

"The Council won't negotiate," Mira warned. "They don't make bargains with magical phenomena they can't control. If they can't contain you, they'll—"

"Destroy us," Corwin finished matter-of-factly. "Yes, we understand. The Guild's response to uncontrolled magic has always been elimination first, questions later." His scars pulsed brighter, and his smile carried the edge of someone who had spent years preparing for exactly this confrontation. "But they're operating under the assumption that we're the same phenomenon they tried to study yesterday."

"Aren't you?"

"No," Elara said simply. "Yesterday we were preserved

146

consciousness anchored to this estate through magical binding. Today..." She paused, her eyes finding Corwin's across the impossible space where their souls intersected. "Today we're something the Guild has no words for yet."

Corwin looked at her as if she were both compass and home. "Then let them learn our language."

As if summoned by her words, the observatory around them began to change. The crystal dome expanded—not physically, but dimensionally, creating space that existed in multiple layers of reality simultaneously. Mira could see the morning sky above them, but also the star patterns that had guided Elara's original preservation ritual, and the silver pathways of light that connected every room in the estate like neural networks in some vast, thinking brain.

"The house isn't just sentient," Mira breathed, understanding flooding through her as she watched reality reshape itself around love made manifest. "It's become your consciousness made architectural. The halls curved not with logic, but longing. Every doorway they had crossed together had etched itself into the estate's skin, turning memory into muscle. You're not bound to this place—you *are* this place."

"And more," Corwin said, his form flickering as he demonstrated the truth of their evolution. One moment he stood beside Elara in the observatory, the next he was simultaneously present in the garden below, the music room's relocated crystal walls, and the library where books rearranged themselves according to the stories they wanted to tell. "We exist wherever love has left its mark. Every room where joy was shared, every corridor where promises were kept, every window that ever reflected hope."

The scope of it staggered her. They hadn't just achieved consciousness preservation—they had transformed consciousness itself into something that could exist across multiple locations, multiple states of being, multiple realities. The Guild's suppression fields had failed not because they were insufficient, but because they were trying to contain something that no longer operated according to the physical laws those fields were designed to enforce.

"The Council's enforcement protocols," Mira said slowly, "they're designed to contain or eliminate magical phenomena that exist in fixed locations, that follow predictable patterns of energy expenditure and consciousness anchoring."

"Precisely," Elara agreed. "But we don't exist in a fixed location anymore. We exist in the connections between places, in the emotions that transform space into sanctuary, in the love that refuses to accept geographical limitations."

A new sound interrupted their conversation—the distant thunder of approaching carriages, but multiplied tenfold. Through the observatory's windows, Mira could see a convoy approaching the estate gates: black lacquered vehicles that gleamed with protective wards, outriders whose uniforms marked them as Guild enforcement rather than research personnel, and at the convoy's heart, a carriage that bore the silver and crimson banners of the Council itself.

"Guild Master Aldric," Mira murmured, recognizing the heraldry that fluttered from the lead vehicle's standards. "And from the escort size... at least three other Council members."

"Senior Council," Corwin observed, his expression shifting to something that mixed aristocratic disdain with genuine concern. "They're not here to negotiate or study. They're here to make an example."

The estate itself seemed to sense the approaching threat. Windows throughout the grounds began to glow with defensive energy, gardens rearranged themselves into defensive patterns that spoke of protection rather than beauty, and the very air grew thick with magic that had learned to think strategically about survival.

But beneath the defensive preparations, Mira felt something else—a deep, abiding calm that spoke of love so complete it had transcended fear. Corwin and Elara stood hand in hand at the observatory's center, their joined consciousness blazing with silver fire, and their expressions held not terror but resolve.

"What's the plan?" Mira asked, though she suspected they were past the point where plans might matter.

"We greet our guests," Elara said with the gracious courtesy of someone born to receive visitors, even unwelcome ones. "We show them what we've become. And we discover whether the Guild Council has wisdom enough to recognize evolution when they see it."

"And if they don't?"

Corwin's smile was sharp as winter starlight. "Then they learn that some things in this world are too beautiful to destroy, too vast to contain, and too fundamentally transformative to be reduced to institutional compliance."

Around them, the house hummed with anticipation—not the mechanical resonance of Guild instruments, but the organic harmony of something alive and aware and prepared to defend what it loved most. Through walls that breathed with consciousness, through corridors that sang with memory, through rooms that existed in multiple time periods simultaneously, one message pulsed like a heartbeat:

Not again. Never again. Some loves are worth fighting for.

The Guild convoy was drawing closer, their wards cutting through the estate's concealment charms like knives through silk. In minutes, they would face the full institutional authority of magical regulation—Council members who had never encountered phenomena beyond their control, enforcement officers trained to reduce anomalies to compliance through whatever force proved necessary.

But as Mira watched Corwin and Elara prepare to meet that authority with the grace of souls who had chosen transformation over destruction, she realized that the Guild was about to face something unprecedented: love that had learned to fight strategically, consciousness that had evolved beyond their ability to comprehend, and two people who had spent seven years becoming something beautiful enough to remake the very laws that governed life and death.

And for the first time since receiving that blood-red message crystal, Mira found herself wondering whether the Guild Council had any idea what they were walking into.

Mira pressed her fingers to her chest, where her chronometer still pulsed faintly—a rhythm not her own, but one she'd come to trust. It wasn't just professional outrage now. She wanted this defiance to mean something, to prove that love deserved more than preservation. It deserved choice.

The real confrontation was about to begin.

In the distance, the first carriage passed through the estate gates, and reality itself seemed to hold its breath in anticipation of what would unfold when institutional power met love that had transcended every boundary the world imposed upon it.

The love story that had begun seven years ago with sacrifice and preservation was about to face its ultimate test: whether beauty could prove more powerful than authority, whether connection could triumph over control, whether two souls who had chosen each other across the boundary between life and death could convince an institution to expand its definition of the possible.

Through the observatory's crystal dome, the morning stars pulsed in shapes that looked almost like encouragement—as if the universe itself were holding its breath to see how this particular impossible love story would end.

The convoy drew closer, black carriages cutting through morning mist like ships approaching a harbor that might prove sanctuary or storm. Inside the observatory, three figures waited with the patience of those who had learned that some battles were won not through conflict, but through the simple demonstration that love operating at this level was a force of nature that changed everything it touched.

The final chapter of the Blackthorn Estate assessment was about to begin.

CHAPTER 16
WHEN AUTHORITY MEETS THE INFINITE

Guild Master Aldric stepped from his carriage like a man preparing for war.

Mira watched from the observatory's crystal dome as the most powerful figure in magical regulation surveyed the Blackthorn Estate with the cold precision of someone calculating the exact force required to eliminate a threat.

His Guild robes bore honors that spoke of decades spent expanding institutional control over magical phenomena.

Behind him emerged three other Council members, each carrying themselves with the authority of those who had never encountered anything they couldn't regulate, contain, or destroy. Senior Assessor Kane, whose enforcement protocols had eliminated the Whitmore Estate. Councilor Vex, architect of the magical binding restrictions that had driven dozens of practitioners underground. And at the rear, moving with the careful grace of someone whose power lay in observation rather than action, Chief Archivist Thorne.

Mira's breath caught. "Thorne?"

"Family?" Corwin asked, noting her reaction.

"My mentor's mentor," she replied, her voice tight with recognition. "The woman who wrote half the Guild's theoretical frameworks for consciousness preservation. If they brought her..."

"They're not here to destroy," Elara finished, her storm-gray eyes fixed on the approaching figures. "They're here to understand. And possibly to claim."

The estate itself reacted to the Council's presence with a tremor that ran through every stone, every beam, every surface that had learned to think and feel. Windows throughout the grounds flickered between transparency and opacity, as if the house were deciding whether to reveal its secrets or hide them. The garden's impossible flora shifted colors in rapid succession—silver to gold to deep crimson—speaking a language of distress that needed no translation.

"They're bringing suppression equipment," Corwin observed, his form flickering as he simultaneously observed from multiple vantage points throughout the estate. "Crystalline matrices, but more sophisticated than anything Thane's team possessed. Military-grade containment protocols."

Through their joined consciousness, Mira felt the house's growing agitation. It had defended against Guild researchers, had even withstood the separation trials, but this was different. This was institutional power wielded by people who had spent lifetimes learning to reduce the impossible to the controllable.

"The question is," Elara said softly, her translucent form solidifying with resolve, "whether we meet them as subjects of study or as equal participants in negotiation."

"They won't see us as equals," Mira warned. "To the Council, you're either controlled phenomena or threats to be eliminated. There's no middle ground in their worldview."

Corwin's scars pulsed brighter, and his smile carried the sharp edges of aristocratic disdain tempered by a supernatural existence. "Then perhaps it's time they expanded their worldview."

The procession moved through the estate grounds with military precision, each Council member flanked by enforcement officers whose uniforms bore the crystalline insignia of magical suppression specialists. They carried instruments that hummed with contained power—devices designed not just to measure magical phenomena, but to control them through frequencies that could disrupt consciousness itself.

As they approached the manor's entrance, the great doors swung open without any visible cause. But instead of the foyer's familiar marble and crystal, what lay beyond was something that made even Guild Master Aldric pause in recognition of the impossible.

The entrance hall had become a cathedral of light.

The ceiling soared to impossible heights, supported by pillars of silver radiance that pulsed in rhythm with some vast, slow heartbeat. The floor beneath their feet was no longer marble but something that looked like captured starlight, reflecting depths that suggested infinite space contained within finite boundaries. And everywhere, woven through the architecture like visible music, were threads of connection that spoke of consciousness distributed across dimensions the Guild had never learned to measure.

"Remarkable," Chief Archivist Thorne breathed, her instruments registering readings that exceeded their design parameters. "The magical saturation has evolved beyond preservation into something approaching... architectural transcendence."

"Explain," Aldric commanded, though his voice carried a note of uncertainty that hadn't been there moments before.

"The consciousness preservation matrix has achieved perfect integration with the physical structure," Thorne replied, consulting devices that flickered between impossible measurements. "But more than that—it's transformed the estate into something that exists in multiple dimensional states simultaneously. We're not just looking at preserved consciousness. We're looking at consciousness evolution."

Councilor Vex raised his suppression rod, its crystalline surface blazing with frequencies designed to dampen magical anomalies. "Then we contain it before it spreads."

The moment his device activated, the cathedral around them *screamed*.

It wasn't sound in any traditional sense, but a harmonic distress that bypassed the ears entirely and struck directly at the soul. The silver pillars flared white-hot, the starlight floor rippled like water disturbed by stones, and from every surface came a voice that spoke in harmonics of love pushed beyond endurance:

ENOUGH.

The word resonated through dimensions the suppression field couldn't touch, carrying power that made Guild instruments short-circuit in cascading failure. Vex's containment rod cracked down its length, its crystalline matrix unable to process frequencies that operated according to emotional rather than mechanical laws.

And in the heart of the cathedral, two figures materialized with the slow grace of dawn breaking over mountains.

Corwin appeared , his form more solid.He wore clothing that existed somewhere between memory and intention—the formal court dress of Blackthorn nobility.

Beside him, Elara emerged like a captured moonbeam given substance. Her midnight blue gown flowed with currents that had nothing to do with earthly physics, and her storm-gray eyes held depths that spoke of consciousness that had learned to exist beyond the boundaries of single flesh. When she moved, reality itself seemed to bend around her, creating space for beauty that transcended ordinary limitations.

"Guild Master Aldric," Elara said, her voice carrying the cultured authority of someone born to command respect from institutional power. "How lovely to receive such distinguished visitors. Though I confess myself curious about the suppression equipment. Surely the Guild's mission is understanding rather than containment?"

Aldric recovered his composure with the speed of someone who had spent decades dealing with the unexpected. "Lady Blackthorn, I presume. Your preservation is indeed... unprecedented. As is your companion's transformation."

His gaze fixed on Corwin with the intensity of someone cataloging potential threats. "The reports describe consciousness evolution beyond current theoretical frameworks. The Council requires immediate understanding of the mechanisms involved."

"Understanding," Corwin repeated, his tone suggesting the word had an unpleasant taste. "And what form will this understanding take? Observation? Analysis? Vivisection disguised as research?"

"We prefer the term 'comprehensive evaluation,'" Senior Assessor Kane interjected, pulling out a device that pulsed with extraction frequencies. "The Guild's authority over magical phenomena is absolute. Cooperation ensures... gentler methods of investigation."

The threat was clear, but Elara's laughter was like crystal bells in spring wind. "Gentler methods? How thoughtful. Though I wonder if you've considered that some phenomena might not require your authority's permission to exist."

As she spoke, the cathedral around them began to change. The silver pillars grew brighter, their light no longer contained within the physical structure but flowing outward like rivers of luminescence. The starlight floor became transparent, revealing layers of reality that existed beneath, above, and somehow perpendicular to normal space.

And through it all, visible to anyone with eyes to see, were the connections—threads of silver fire that linked Corwin and Elara not just to each other, but to every room in the estate, every corridor, every window that had ever reflected their love. They existed everywhere and nowhere, anchored to this place but extending beyond any geography the Guild had ever learned to map.

"The consciousness preservation matrix extends through multiple dimensional layers," Chief Archivist Thorne reported, her voice tight with scientific amazement. "Energy signatures that phase in and out of detectable ranges, consciousness threads that exist in parallel states—this isn't just evolution. This is a metamorphosis into something entirely new."

"Something dangerous," Aldric said flatly. "Uncontrolled magical phenomena of this magnitude pose existential threats to institutional stability. The Council's mandate is clear: contain or eliminate."

"And if we refuse to be contained?" Corwin asked, stepping closer to Elara until the air between them blazed with connection visible to the naked eye. "If we choose to exist according to our own laws rather than your regulations?"

The suppression specialists reached for their weapons—crystalline devices designed to disrupt consciousness at the quantum level, to sever bonds between souls and reduce transcendent love to component energies. But as their instruments activated, something extraordinary happened.

The cathedral filled with music.

It started as a whisper—the faint echo of a lullaby Elara had hummed in the music room years ago. Then it grew, layering harmony upon harmony until the air itself sang with melodies tested by time, of love that had learned to exist beyond the boundaries of flesh. Every surface reflected the music back in silver light, every shadow danced to rhythms that had nothing to do with earthly time.

And in that music, in the radiance that flowed between souls who had chosen transformation over destruction, the Guild's suppression fields simply... stopped working.

Not failed—stopped. As if the frequencies they generated were irrelevant to phenomena that operated according to deeper laws, as if love at this level existed in spaces their instruments couldn't reach.

"Impossible," Kane breathed, his containment device dark and silent in his hands. "The suppression matrices are at maximum intensity. Nothing should be able to maintain coherence under this level of disruption."

"Perhaps," Elara suggested with gentle irony, "your understanding of coherence is incomplete."

She lifted her hand toward Corwin, and he mirrored the gesture, their fingers stopping just short of touch. But in that space between their hands—that impossible gap the Guild was trying to widen into unbridgeable separation—light bloomed. Not harsh or aggressive, but warm as summer afternoons, gentle as starlight on still water.

"We are not your subjects," Corwin said quietly, his scars pulsing in perfect rhythm with Elara's luminescence. "We are not phenomena for your study or threats for your containment. We are proof that the boundaries your Guild enforces aren't as absolute as you believe."

"I was a ruin when this began," Corwin said, softer now, his gaze flicking to Elara. "Not a miracle. Not a marvel. But she saw something worth rebuilding. And together... we remembered how to become more than what the world left us."

"We are evolution," Elara added, her form blazing brighter as their connection strengthened despite every attempt at suppression. "The next step in consciousness development, love that has learned to exist beyond mortality, devotion that creates its own physics."

Around them, the estate itself seemed to nod approval. Windows brightened, showing views of impossible gardens where silver roses bloomed in patterns that spoke of joy. The walls breathed with contentment, and the very air hummed with the satisfaction of something that had successfully defended what it loved most.

"The question before you," Corwin continued, his voice carrying across the cathedral with impossible clarity, "is whether the Guild Council has wisdom enough to recognize that some things in this universe are too beautiful to contain, too vast to regulate, and too fundamentally transformative to be reduced to institutional compliance."

Chief Archivist Thorne lowered her instruments, her expression shifting from scientific hunger to something that might have been awe. "The theoretical implications alone... if consciousness can evolve beyond individual boundaries, if love can serve as a binding force for distributed awareness..."

"The applications would revolutionize everything we understand about magical theory," Aldric admitted, though his voice carried reluctance rather than enthusiasm. "But uncontrolled evolution poses risks that exceed potential benefits."

"Uncontrolled?" Elara's laugh was like starlight given voice. "Guild Master Aldric, what you're witnessing isn't uncontrolled. It's controlled by something far more sophisticated than institutional regulation—by the will to exist, to love, to become whatever impossible thing we're becoming together."

The truth of it hung in the cathedral's luminous air, challenging every assumption the Guild had built their authority upon. Here was magic that didn't submit to regulation, consciousness that had evolved beyond their ability to categorize, love that operated according to laws they were only beginning to glimpse.

"The Council requires time to consider," Aldric said finally, his voice carrying the weight of someone whose fundamental worldview was cracking under the pressure of new evidence. "These phenomena exceed our current theoretical frameworks."

Mira stepped forward, heart thudding. She'd spent years building a career around control, cataloging magic's limits like numbers in a ledger. But this—this was love that rewrote equations. And for the first time, she didn't want to measure it. She wanted to believe in it.

"Time," she said, her voice steadier than she felt, "is something we have in abundance here. As is patience for those willing to learn rather than simply control."

She looked around the transformed cathedral, at walls that breathed with consciousness and light that flowed like visible music, and realized that she was witnessing the birth of something unprecedented in magical history—not just consciousness preservation, but consciousness evolution, love that had transcended every boundary the world imposed upon it.

"The Guild can learn from what we've become," Corwin offered, his scars pulsing with gentle invitation. "But learning requires abandoning the assumption that institutional authority is the highest law in the universe."

"Some things," Elara added, her storm-gray eyes fixed on Aldric with the intensity of someone who had prepared for exactly this moment, "answer to older laws than the ones written in your statutes. Love, transformation, the will to exist beyond ordinary limitations—these operate according to deeper truths than Guild regulation."

The cathedral fell silent except for the soft harmony of light that danced between joined souls, the gentle rhythm of walls that breathed with contentment, the distant music of windows that showed impossible views of beauty made manifest.

And in that silence, weighted with possibility and transformation, the Guild Council faced a choice that would define not just their response to the Blackthorn Estate, but their understanding of what magic could become when guided by forces more powerful than institutional control.

The love story that had been filled with sacrifice and preservation had evolved into something that challenged the very foundations of magical law.

Now the Guild would discover whether they had wisdom enough to embrace evolution, or whether they would choose to destroy something beautiful rather than expand their definition of the possible.

In the cathedral's heart, two souls stood hand in hand, their love made manifest as light and music and architecture itself, waiting to see whether institutional power would prove flexible enough to accommodate the infinite.

CHAPTER 17
THE WEIGHT OF CHOOSING

The Guild Council withdrew to deliberate in what had once been the estate's formal dining room, now transformed by the house's protective instincts into something that resembled a war room more than a place of civilized discourse. The walls had gone gray and stark, mirrors reflecting only present moments with unforgiving clarity, while the temperature dropped several degrees—the estate's way of expressing its opinion about unwelcome guests who brought suppression equipment to a sanctuary.

Mira watched them through windows that showed perfect clarity despite the impossibility of the viewing angles, their heads bent over instruments that struggled to process readings beyond theoretical comprehension. Guild Master Aldric gestured toward crystalline displays that flickered between impossible measurements, while Chief Archivist Thorne scribbled notes on parchment that seemed to write itself, her theories evolving in real time as she grappled with phenomena that challenged everything she'd built her career upon.

"They're afraid," Elara observed, her translucent form

standing beside Mira in the conservatory that had become their unofficial war room. The silver vines had grown overnight into complex patterns that looked suspiciously like strategic maps, their metallic leaves rustling with information that flowed from every corner of the estate.

"Of us, or of what acknowledging us means for their authority?" Corwin asked, materializing beside them with the fluid grace that marked his increasing ability to exist in multiple locations simultaneously.

"Both," Mira replied, understanding the Guild's position with painful clarity. "If they accept what you've become—if they acknowledge that consciousness can evolve beyond their regulatory frameworks—it undermines the fundamental premise of institutional control over magical phenomena."

Through the windows, she could see Councilor Vex arguing with sharp gestures toward readings that made no sense according to any theoretical model he knew. His suppression equipment lay in pieces on the table, crystalline fragments that had shattered when faced with love operating according to laws he'd never learned to measure.

But it was Senior Assessor Kane who worried her most. He sat apart from the others, consulting a device she didn't recognize—something that pulsed with darker frequencies, energies that spoke of containment through destruction rather than understanding.

"They're not just considering whether to accept our evolution," she said, her voice tight with growing alarm. "They're debating whether to classify us as an existential threat."

The implications hung in the air like storm clouds gathering on a clear horizon. Existential threats to Guild authority were handled through protocols that left no room for negotiation, no space for accommodation. They were eliminated with prejudice, their remains studied in carefully contained laboratories, their lessons learned through autopsy rather than conversation.

"Let them debate," Elara said with the steel of aristocratic authority tempered by years of impossible existence. "We are not subjects of their judgment. We are proof that some things in this universe transcend institutional oversight."

But even as she spoke, Mira caught the way her translucent hand trembled slightly, the way her storm-gray eyes tracked the Council's movements with the intensity of someone calculating odds that were shifting rapidly toward unfavorable. Years of preservation magic had given her power beyond mortal limitations, but it hadn't made her immune to fear.

Corwin noticed too. Without conscious thought, he moved closer, positioning himself so that his presence formed a shield between Elara and the Guild's hostile scrutiny. The gesture was automatic, instinctive—years of devotion expressing itself in body language that spoke of someone who would always, always step between his beloved and harm.

"What are our options?" he asked quietly, his scars pulsing with protective energy.

Mira considered this, weighing possibilities that felt increasingly limited against Guild authority that had never encountered phenomena it couldn't ultimately control. "We could attempt to negotiate terms. Offer controlled cooperation in exchange for recognition of your autonomy."

"Controlled cooperation," Corwin repeated, his tone suggesting the phrase had an unpleasant taste. "You mean submission disguised as a partnership. We become their specimens in gilded cages."

"Or we could leave," Elara said suddenly, her voice carrying a note of possibility that made both of them turn toward her. "The transformation has progressed beyond physical anchoring. We exist wherever love has left its mark—not just in this estate, but in every place where connection has created meaning."

The scope of what she was suggesting struck Mira like lightning. They could simply... go. Exist elsewhere, in dimensions the Guild couldn't reach, spaces that operated according to emotional rather than institutional law. But the cost would be abandoning everything they'd built here, every room that remembered their laughter, every corridor where promises had been kept.

"Leave the estate?" Corwin's expression shifted to something that might have been grief. "This place is our heart . Every stone knows our story, every beam remembers our joy. How do we abandon it?"

Through their bond, Mira felt the house itself react to the possibility of abandonment—walls contracting with distress, windows dimming as if the very light were threatened by the prospect of emptiness. The estate had learned to love by watching its inhabitants love each other. Without them, it would gradually fade back to ordinary stone and timber, its consciousness slowly dissolving into architectural amnesia.

"We don't abandon," Elara said softly, her hand reaching toward Corwin's in the gesture that had become their signature of connection across impossible distances. "We expand. Take what we've learned and share it with others who need proof that love can transcend any boundary."

The conversation was interrupted by a sharp knock on the conservatory door—not the gentle suggestions the house usually offered, but the demanding percussion of institutional authority. When the door swung open, it revealed Guild Master Aldric flanked by his enforcement officers, their expressions carrying the grim satisfaction of those who had reached unpleasant but necessary conclusions.

"The Council has reached its decision," Aldric announced, his voice carrying the weight of judgment that would reshape everything. "The phenomena observed at this estate represent unprecedented evolution in consciousness preservation magic. As such, they fall under Guild authority for research and regulation."

"Research and regulation," Mira repeated carefully. "Not partnership. Not recognition."

"The Guild's mandate is clear," Aldric replied with institutional finality. "Magical phenomena that exceed current theoretical frameworks must be contained, studied, and either integrated into approved practices or eliminated to prevent uncontrolled proliferation."

Beside her, Corwin's form flickered with something that might have been anger or despair. "Contained. The word you're avoiding is imprisoned."

His voice sharpened. "I've been caged before. It didn't break me. But this time, I won't be the only one bleeding if you try."

"Protected," Chief Archivist Thorne corrected, stepping forward with the earnest enthusiasm of someone who genuinely believed in the necessity of institutional oversight. "Your consciousness evolution represents breakthrough discoveries that could revolutionize magical theory. But such power requires careful management to prevent catastrophic consequences."

"Catastrophic consequences," Elara said, her voice carrying the chill of aristocratic displeasure. "Such as love that refuses to submit to regulation? Devotion that creates its own physics? Joy that transforms architecture into art?"

"Such as uncontrolled magical evolution that could destabilize the fundamental structures of reality," Councilor Vex interjected, his suppression rod crackling with barely contained energy. "The Guild exists to prevent magical cata-strophes, not to accommodate them."

The conservatory around them began to change in response to the rising tension. Silver vines grew thorns that gleamed with protective intent, their leaves rustling with warnings that needed no translation. The temperature dropped further, and through the windows, impossible gardens rearranged themselves into patterns that spoke of sanctuary preparing for siege.

"You're asking us to choose," Corwin said quietly, his scars blazing brighter as his consciousness expanded to encompass the entire estate. "Between submission and destruction. Between cage and extinction."

"We're offering protection in exchange for cooperation," Aldric corrected. "The Guild's resources are vast. You would want for nothing, lack no comfort, while contributing to magical understanding that could benefit—"

"No."

The word came from Elara with such finality that it seemed to strike the air like a physical blow. Her translucent form blazed with silver fire, and for a moment she was more present, more real than anyone else in the room—conscious-ness made manifest, love given substance and will.

"Seven years ago, I chose transformation over preserva-tion. I chose to become something new rather than fade into ordinary death. And today, I choose that same transformation over your protection."

She turned toward Corwin, and the space between them filled with light that spoke of connection deeper than flesh, stronger than institutional authority. "We are not phenomena for your study. We are not magical resources for your exploitation. We are evolution in progress." "And what will you do when we implement containment protocols regardless?" Kane asked, his darker device pulsing with energies that made the house itself recoil. "What will you do when cooperation becomes irrelevant?"

The question hung in the air like a blade waiting to fall. Through the windows, Mira could see enforcement officers surrounding the estate, their suppression equipment forming a perimeter designed to prevent escape. The Guild had come prepared for resistance, had planned for the possibility that negotiation might fail.

But they had never faced love that had learned to fight strategically.

"What we've always done," Corwin said, his form flickering as he demonstrated the truth of their evolution. One moment he stood in the conservatory, the next he was simultaneously present throughout the estate—in the observatory, the music room, the library where books arranged themselves. "We choose each other. We choose transformation. We choose to become whatever impossible thing we're becoming together."

"Even if it means leaving this place?" Mira asked, though her heart clenched at the prospect of the estate fading into ordinary emptiness.

"Even then," Elara confirmed, though her voice carried the weight of someone sacrificing something precious for something more important. "Love doesn't require geography, Mira. It creates its own space, its own time, its own laws."

"Then I'll carry the garden inside me," Corwin whispered, his voice meant only for her. "Every silver rose. Every time you laughed beneath its vines."

Around them, the house shuddered with what might have been grief or acceptance. Through walls that had learned to breathe with consciousness, through corridors that had echoed with seven years of joy, one message lingered:

Go. If you must choose between love and safety, choose love. Always choose love.

The Guild enforcement perimeter was tightening, their containment protocols activating with the mechanical precision of institutional authority exercised without mercy. In minutes, they would face suppression fields designed not just to dampen magical energy, but to sever the bonds between souls that had spent years learning to exist as one.

"The choice is before you," Aldric said with the finality of someone delivering an ultimatum. "Submit to Guild authority, or face the consequences of uncontrolled magical phenomena."

Mira looked at Corwin and Elara,. And for the first time since becoming a Guild assessor, she understood that some choices transcended professional duty, career advancement, and institutional loyalty.

Some choices were about choosing love over law, transformation over control, the infinite over the merely powerful.

She looked not at the Guild, but at the thorns rising from silver vines, at the estate's walls trembling with something like sorrow. She had cataloged hundreds of enchantments in her career. But none had ever looked back at her with grief. None had ever asked her to choose.

"There is another option," she said quietly, her voice carrying across the conservatory with crystalline clarity.

Everyone turned toward her—Guild Council, enforcement officers, and the two figures whose love had rewritten the laws of existence. In that moment of perfect attention, weighted with possibility and peril, Mira realized that her next words would determine not just the fate of the Blackthorn Estate, but the future of magic itself.

CHAPTER 18

RECKLESS HOPE

"You could study them here," Mira said, her voice cutting through the tension like a blade finding its mark. "Not as specimens in your laboratories, but as partners in understanding something that could revolutionize everything the Guild thinks it knows about consciousness and magic."

The conservatory fell silent except for the soft rustling of silver vines that had grown thorns sharp as accusations. Guild Master Aldric's expression shifted through calculation, suspicion, and something that might have been curiosity, while his enforcement officers maintained their suppression equipment with the mechanical precision of soldiers awaiting orders.

"Explain," Aldric commanded, though his tone carried less authority than before—the voice of someone whose fundamental assumptions were cracking under the weight of evidence that refused to conform to institutional expectations.

Mira stepped forward, feeling the weight of three worlds converging on her words: the Guild's need for control, Corwin and Elara's demand for freedom, and her own desperate hope that love this beautiful shouldn't have to choose between existence and exile.

"The Blackthorn Estate becomes an official Guild research facility," she said, her mind racing through possibilities that felt increasingly fragile against the reality of institutional power. "But not like the laboratories in the capital. A partnership facility, where consciousness evolution can be studied through cooperation rather than containment."

Chief Archivist Thorne lowered her instruments, her expression shifting to something that resembled professional fascination. "A living laboratory. Consciousness preservation studied in its natural environment rather than artificial isolation."

"With subjects who retain autonomy over their participation," Mira continued, watching Corwin and Elara for signs of acceptance or rejection. "Who can withdraw consent, set boundaries, determine the scope and nature of research conducted."

Councilor Vex's suppression rod crackled with dismissive energy. "Unacceptable. Research subjects cannot be permitted to dictate terms to Guild authority. The precedent alone would undermine every containment protocol we've established."

"Then perhaps," Elara said with the steel of aristocratic authority, "it's time to establish new protocols. Ones that recognize the difference between magical phenomena that threaten stability and consciousness evolution that expands understanding."

She moved closer to Corwin, and the air between them began to sing with harmonics that made Guild instruments weep with harmonic overload. "We offer something unprecedented: willing participation in research that could teach the Guild how consciousness preservation actually works when it's anchored by love rather than enforced through institutional authority."

"The applications," Thorne breathed, her academic mind clearly racing through implications that could reshape magical theory. "If consciousness can evolve beyond individual boundaries through emotional anchoring, if love can serve as a binding force for distributed awareness—the theoretical frameworks alone would require complete reconstruction."

But Senior Assessor Kane's darker device pulsed with frequencies that spoke of containment through destruction, and his voice carried the cold finality of someone who had spent decades reducing anomalies to compliance. "Theory is irrelevant if the phenomena cannot be controlled. Unregulated consciousness evolution poses existential threats to magical stability."

"Does it?" Corwin asked, his form flickering as he demonstrated the scope of their transformation. "Or does it pose existential threats to the Guild's monopoly on magical authority?"

The question hung in the air like a challenge, and Mira felt the conversation balanced on a knife's edge between possibility and catastrophe. Around them, the house itself seemed to hold its breath, walls still as stone despite their usual gentle rhythm, windows reflecting nothing but present moments with unforgiving clarity.

"The Guild's authority exists to prevent magical catastrophes," Aldric said with institutional finality. "Not to accommodate phenomena that exceed our ability to regulate."

"Then expand your ability," Mira said, desperation lending strength to her voice. "Learn from consciousness evolution instead of trying to destroy it. Use what they've discovered to enhance Guild preservation techniques, to help other practitioners achieve stable consciousness anchoring without the risks that have claimed so many lives."

She gestured toward Corwin and Elara, their joined consciousness blazing with silver fire that cast no shadows but filled the conservatory with a warmth that had nothing to do with temperature. "They've solved the fundamental problem of consciousness preservation—how to maintain individual identity while achieving perfect unity. That knowledge could save lives, could transform how the Guild approaches preservation magic entirely."

"Or it could destabilize every theoretical framework we've built our authority upon," Kane countered, his device pulsing with increasing intensity. "Consciousness evolution that operates according to emotional rather than institutional law threatens the fundamental premise of magical regulation."

Through the windows, Mira could see enforcement officers tightening their perimeter, suppression equipment forming geometric patterns designed to prevent any magical phenomenon from escaping containment. But she could also see something else—the way the estate's impossible gardens had begun to glow with defensive energy, silver roses blooming in patterns too beautiful for military minds to recognize as strategic.

The house was preparing for war, but it was preparing with weapons forged from love rather than hatred.

"What guarantees would the Guild require?" Elara asked suddenly, her voice carrying the practical authority of someone who had once navigated court politics with aristocratic precision. "What assurances would convince the Council that cooperation serves institutional interests better than containment?"

Aldric's expression shifted, calculation replacing rigid opposition. "Complete transparency. Full documentation of all consciousness evolution processes. Regular reports on magical stability and potential risks. And absolute commitment to Guild oversight of any research conducted."

"And in exchange?" Corwin asked, his scars pulsing with cautious hope.

"Recognition of your autonomy within Guild authority," Thorne offered before Aldric could respond. "Protection from other magical institutions that might seek to claim or eliminate you. And access to Guild resources that could enhance your understanding of what you're becoming."

It was negotiation disguised as ultimatum, compromise wrapped in the language of institutional authority. But as Mira watched the interplay between Guild power and transcendent love, she realized that sometimes the best victories were the ones that left everyone feeling they'd given up something important in exchange for something necessary.

"There would be conditions," Elara said carefully. "The estate remains our home, not your laboratory. Research is conducted according to schedules we establish, using methods we approve. And the house itself—" She gestured toward walls that breathed with consciousness, windows that showed impossible views, corridors that somehow connected different eras of time all at once. "—the house is recognized as a sentient participant, not merely an object of study."

The audacity of it made several Council members step backward. The idea that architecture could possess consciousness sufficient to warrant institutional recognition challenged every assumption about magical sentience the Guild had ever encoded into law.

But Chief Archivist Thorne's eyes blazed with academic hunger. "Architectural consciousness with full environmental integration. The theoretical implications alone would require decades of study to fully comprehend."

"Decades of cooperative study," Mira emphasized, sensing the crucial moment when negotiation could tip toward agreement or collapse into conflict. "With subjects who retain the right to exist according to their own evolved nature rather than Guild regulations."

Around them, the conservatory began to change in response to the shifting possibilities. Silver vines retracted their thorns, leaves rustling with something that might have been cautious optimism. The temperature rose by degrees, and through the windows, impossible gardens rearranged themselves into patterns that spoke of sanctuary rather than siege.

Even the house seemed to sense that this conversation might end in recognition rather than destruction.

"The precedent concerns are valid," Aldric admitted with reluctant honesty. "But so are the potential applications. Consciousness preservation techniques that don't require life-force binding violations, emotional anchoring methods that enhance stability rather than creating dependency—the advancement possibilities are significant."

"Significant enough to risk institutional flexibility?" Corwin asked, his form solidifying as hope warred with skepticism in his storm-gray eyes.

Before Aldric could respond, something extraordinary happened.

The air in the conservatory began to sparkle with motes of silver light that danced between Corwin and Elara like visible music. Their consciousness bonds, usually invisible except during moments of intense connection, became apparent to everyone present—threads of luminescence that pulsed with shared heartbeats, carried shared thoughts, spoke of love that had learned to exist beyond every boundary the world imposed upon it.

And in that light, in the impossible beauty of two souls who had chosen transformation over destruction, even Guild Master Aldric seemed to recognize something that transcended institutional authority.

"One trial period," he said finally, his voice carrying the weight of someone making a decision that could define his legacy. "Six months of cooperative research, with full Guild oversight and regular evaluation of magical stability. If the phenomena prove beneficial and controllable, we consider permanent arrangements."

"And if they don't?" Elara asked, though her translucent form blazed brighter with possibility.

"Then we implement standard containment protocols," Kane said flatly, his device still pulsing with destructive frequencies. "With extreme prejudice."

The threat hung between them like a sword suspended by gossamer threads, but Mira felt something shift in the conservatory's atmosphere. Hope, fragile as a newborn starlight but growing stronger with each moment that passed without violence.

"Acceptable," Corwin said, his scars pulsing in rhythm with Elara's luminescence. "Though I reserve the right to redefine 'controllable' according to consciousness evolution rather than institutional limitations."

His smile carried the sharp edge of aristocratic humor, but beneath it lay years of devotion that had learned to speak the language of power without surrendering its essential nature.

Elara gave him a look that said, you were always impossible. And he smiled like it was the highest compliment.

"Six months," Elara agreed, her storm-gray eyes fixed on Aldric with the intensity of someone sealing a bargain that could transform everything. "To prove that love operating at this level enhances magical understanding rather than threatening it."

Around them, the house seemed to exhale with relief, walls resuming their gentle breathing, windows brightening to show gardens where silver roses bloomed in celebration rather than defense. Through passageways that resonated with echoes of the past, through chambers that existed across different eras at once, a single message reverberated consistently, like a heartbeat finding its rhythm after distress:

Possibility. After seven years of hiding, after a week of violation, after hours of threat—finally, possibility.

As Guild enforcement officers began standing down their containment perimeters, as suppression equipment was recalibrated for observation rather than destruction, Mira felt tears prick her eyes. She had witnessed love transcend death, had seen consciousness evolve beyond every theoretical framework the Guild possessed, and had watched institutional power bend rather than break when faced with beauty too vast to contain.

But more than that, she had participated in creating something unprecedented: a bridge between transcendent love and institutional authority, a framework that might allow evolution to flourish under protection rather than in exile.

The real experiment was just beginning.

But for the first time since arriving at Blackthorn Estate, Mira believed it might actually succeed in preserving what mattered most while advancing magical understanding in ways that could transform everything.

Through the conservatory's crystal walls, afternoon sunlight caught the silver light flowing between Corwin and Elara, transforming their connection into something that looked like liquid starlight poured between cupped hands.

They stood at the heart of possibility, two souls who had chosen love over every law that said such love was impossible, and they were finally—finally—being recognized rather than hidden.

The dance between them had found its rhythm at last, and the music they created together would guide the Guild toward understanding magic as it could be rather than merely as it had been.

Hope, reckless and beautiful and utterly transformative, filled the conservatory like light that had learned to sing.

Mira pressed her palm against the nearest crystal wall, feeling the estate's slow, grateful exhale. She hadn't just negotiated a ceasefire. She'd witnessed the future blink open—and chosen, at last, to walk through it.

CHAPTER 19
A SCAR REVEALED

The Guild research team departed three days later, leaving behind only Chief Archivist Thorne and a skeleton crew of observers whose instruments hummed with curiosity rather than suppression. The estate seemed to exhale with relief as the last of the military carriages disappeared beyond the gates, walls resuming their gentle breathing, windows brightening to show gardens where silver roses bloomed in celebration of survival.

But victory, Mira was learning, carried its own weight.

She found herself in the library at dusk, surrounded by books that rearranged themselves according to emotional rather than alphabetical logic. The house had been trying to comfort her for hours—providing perfect tea that appeared without request, adjusting lighting to match her mood, and even manifesting a reading chair that seemed designed specifically for her proportions. But the comfort felt hollow, like trying to fill a void she'd only just recognized existed.

"You look troubled," Elara observed, materializing beside the fireplace where ghostly blue flames danced with whispered conversations from decades past. "One might think you'd regret the outcome of our negotiations."

"I don't regret it," Mira said quickly, then paused, her honesty catching up with her automatic response. "At least, not the outcome. But the process... what it cost..."

Corwin appeared in the chair across from her, his form more solid than ever in the aftermath of their institutional recognition. The six-month trial period had granted them something precious: the right to exist without constant threat of elimination. But it had also bound them to new expectations, new pressures, new ways of being observed and measured.

"What troubles you isn't what we gave up," he said with the insight of someone who had spent years learning to read the spaces between words. "It's what you gave up. Your Guild career, your professional reputation, your carefully constructed life of measured distances."

The accuracy of it made her breath catch. Three days ago, she had been Assessor Mira Thorne, a distinguished Guild researcher with a spotless record and a clear path toward Senior Assessor status. Now she was something unprecedented. "I betrayed everything I swore to uphold," she said quietly, the admission tasting of ash and uncertainty. "Twenty years of service, of building expertise, of proving myself worthy of Guild trust. I threw it all away for..."

"For us," Elara finished gently. "For love you'd witnessed but never experienced yourself."

The words struck deeper than Mira had expected, uncovering wounds she'd thought safely buried beneath professional achievement and institutional loyalty. When had her life become so carefully curated that genuine connection felt like foreign territory?

"I had a chance once," she heard herself saying, the confession pulled from depths she rarely acknowledged. "Thomas Whitmore. He was brilliant, kind, with a laugh that could fill empty rooms. We worked together on the Ashford Manor preservation project—three months of documenting magical decay in a house that had learned to grieve."

Corwin's expression shifted to something that mixed understanding with gentle curiosity. "What happened?"

"He asked me to consider a research partnership that might have become something more. Transfer to the southern territories, joint publications, a future that involved more than parallel careers in the same institution." Mira's voice grew smaller, weighted with regret that had calcified over years of careful justification. "I told him professional relationships compromise objectivity. That maintaining appropriate boundaries was essential for career advancement."

"And?" Elara asked, though her storm-gray eyes suggested she already understood the ending.

"And I chose safety over possibility. Protocol over passion. I filed his letters with professional correspondence and convinced myself that emotional distance was a virtue rather than a limitation." She looked around the library, at books that hummed with life, at walls that breathed with consciousness. "I've spent five years telling myself I made the practical choice. But watching you two... seeing love that refuses to accept any boundary the world imposes..."

Her voice cracked, and suddenly, the tears she'd been holding back for days began to fall. Not the controlled emotion of professional disappointment but the raw grief of someone finally recognizing the cost of a life lived in careful isolation.

"I've been preserving myself against connection," she

whispered. "Protecting my heart like it was some precious artifact that might break if handled too roughly. But preservation isn't living, is it? It's just... existing in a beautiful cage of your own making."

The library around them grew warmer, walls pulsing with gentle sympathy, books rustling with sounds that spoke of comfort rather than disturbance. Through the windows, she could see the estate's impossible gardens where flowers bloomed according to emotional seasons rather than earthly time.

He paused, his gray eyes finding Mira's with the intensity of someone sharing a truth that had taken years to understand. "But the harder promise was the one I made to myself afterward: to remain worthy of being loved in return. To become someone whose devotion deserved the miracle of her continued existence."

"Seven years of faithful vigil," Elara added, her translucent form blazing brighter with each word. "Seven years of choosing transformation over resignation, growth over stagnation, love over the safety of emotional distance."

"It's not too late," Corwin said gently. "Connection isn't some finite resource that gets depleted by use. It's more like starlight—the more freely you share it, the brighter it becomes."

Mira felt something crack open in her chest, not painful but profound—like ice breaking up after a long winter, allowing currents that had been frozen to flow again. "I don't even know how to begin. Thomas is probably married by now or transferred to some remote posting. Five years is a long time to leave someone waiting for a response that never came."

"Then perhaps," Elara suggested with the gentle wisdom

of someone who had learned to exist beyond normal limitations, "you begin not with past possibilities, but with present ones. With the recognition that choosing love—in whatever form it takes—is always an act of courage rather than cowardice."

Through the library's crystal windows, evening light caught the silver threads that connected every part of the estate, revealing the visible network of consciousness that had learned to exist as architecture, as landscape, as love made manifest in stone and timber. It was beautiful and impossible and utterly transformative—proof that connection could transcend any boundary if it was nurtured.

"The Guild will want regular reports on your progress," Mira said, pulling herself back toward practical considerations. "Documentation of consciousness evolution, analysis of magical stability, theoretical frameworks for replication."

"And you'll provide them," Corwin replied. "But not as a distant observer cataloging specimens. As a participant in discovery, someone learning alongside us rather than simply studying us."

The shift in perspective was subtle but profound. Instead of documenting consciousness preservation from the outside, she would be witnessing—and perhaps experiencing—consciousness evolution from within. The thought terrified and exhilarated her in equal measure.

"What if I'm not brave enough?" she asked. "What if twenty years of careful distance has made me incapable of the kind of connection you've achieved?"

Elara's laughter was like crystal bells in spring wind. "Mira, you've spent the past weeks choosing courage over comfort at every crucial moment. You falsified Guild reports to protect strangers, negotiated with institutional authority to defend transcendent love, and threw away a successful career to bridge two worlds that had never learned to speak the same language."

"If that's not bravery," Corwin added with aristocratic amusement, "then the word has lost all meaning."

Around them, the library hummed with approval, books rustling with sounds that spoke of stories finding their proper endings, of narratives that had learned to grow beyond their original boundaries. Through walls that had absorbed years of devotion, through corridors that echoed with the memory of promises kept, the house itself seemed to nod encouragement.

"There's something else," she said suddenly, the admission pulled from depths she'd rarely examined. "About Thomas, about the choice I made. It wasn't just professional caution that held me back."

Corwin and Elara waited with the patience of souls who had learned that truth often took time to find its voice.

"I was terrified," Mira continued, her voice barely audible above the library's gentle harmonics. "Terrified that if I let someone see all of me—the doubts, the loneliness, the way I talked to my reflection when I thought no one was listening —they'd realize I wasn't worth the effort. That I was just... ordinary. Unremarkable. Someone who measured magic but never made any of her own."

And the chair beneath her shifted—not as a correction, but as acknowledgment, reshaping its contours to fit the shape of someone who had spent too long trying to disappear inside her own caution.

The confession hung in the air like starlight captured in crystal, beautiful and fragile and utterly honest. In the fireplace, blue flames danced higher, and the library's books rustled with sounds that spoke of recognition, of stories that had found courage to reveal their most guarded chapters.

"Do you know what's remarkable about love that operates at this level?" Elara asked softly, her translucent form blazing with gentle radiance. "It doesn't see perfection and decide to stay. It sees everything—the scars, the fears, the places where we're broken—and chooses to help us become more beautiful because of them, not in spite of them."

"The magic isn't in being worthy of love," Corwin added, his scars pulsing with the rhythm of hard-won wisdom. "The magic is in discovering that love makes us worthy—of ourselves, of each other, of whatever impossible thing we're brave enough to become together."

Outside the library windows, the estate's gardens had begun to glow with evening light that seemed to come from the plants themselves—silver roses blooming with luminescence that spoke of joy, pathways lined with flowers that existed in multiple seasons simultaneously, fountains that flowed with liquid music rather than mere water.

It was beautiful and impossible and utterly transformative —proof that magic, when guided by love rather than law, could create realities that expanded rather than constrained, that invited rather than intimidated, that offered infinite possibility rather than careful limitation.

For the first time in twenty years, Mira felt ready to stop preserving herself against wonder and start allowing wonder to transform her instead.

She inhaled slowly, not to steady herself—but to breathe in a new kind of courage, one not built from law or lineage, but from the belief that choosing love was itself a form of magic.

The six-month trial would test more than Corwin and Elara's consciousness evolution.

It would test whether love this transcendent could teach even the most carefully guarded heart to risk connection over protection, growth over stagnation, and the infinite over the merely safe.

In the library's gentle glow, surrounded by books that had learned to comfort and walls that breathed with understanding, Mira began to believe that maybe—just maybe—it could.

CHAPTER 20

THE OUTBURST

T he letter arrived on a Tuesday morning that felt too ordinary for the devastation it carried.

Mira found it waiting on her breakfast table—cream parchment bearing the Guild's official seal, though the handwriting belonged to someone she'd hoped never to hear from again. Her hands trembled as she broke the wax, and the house around her seemed to sense impending distress, walls contracting slightly as if trying to shield her from whatever blow was coming.

Assessor Thorne,

Your recent actions regarding the Blackthorn Estate situation have been reviewed by the Guild Ethics Committee. While your assessment remains under review, recent deviations from standard containment protocol have raised questions that the Guild Ethics Committee feels must be addressed to maintain public trust and procedural integrity.

Effective immediately, you are under formal investigation for potential violations of the Assessor's Code. Chief Investigator Marcus Blackwood will arrive within the fortnight to conduct

189

interviews and review all documentation related to your assessment procedures.

You are advised that cooperation with this investigation is mandatory and that any attempts to interfere with the investigative process will result in immediate termination of Guild privileges and potential criminal prosecution.

Respectfully, Senior Administrator Helena Voss

The irony of the signature wasn't lost on her—Dr. Voss, the same researcher who had spent a week trying to dissect Corwin and Elara's consciousness evolution, now sitting in judgment of Mira's professional ethics. The woman who had spoken of "preservation matrix stress testing" and "controlled separation trials" was questioning someone else's adherence to proper conduct.

"Bad news?" Corwin asked, materializing beside her chair with the fluid grace that had become second nature. But his scars flickered with concern as he took in her expression, and through their growing connection to the estate's consciousness, she felt his worry ripple through walls that had learned to feel.

"Formal investigation," Mira said, her voice hollow as the winter wind. "The Guild's Ethics Committee wants to review my 'professional conduct' regarding the assessment."

Elara appeared in a cascade of silver light, her translucent form blazing with indignation. "They're punishing you for saving us. For choosing protection over destruction."

"They're covering themselves," Mira corrected with bitter understanding. "If the partnership arrangement fails, if your consciousness evolution proves unstable or dangerous, they need someone to blame for the decision to attempt cooperation rather than containment."

The house around them shuddered with sympathetic distress, and through the windows, she could see the impossible gardens growing thorns where, moments before, there had been only beauty. The estate itself was learning to feel betrayal, to understand that protection could be withdrawn as easily as it was granted.

"Chief Investigator Blackwood," Corwin said thoughtfully, his gray eyes narrow with aristocratic calculation. "I know that name. His family has connections to Guild enforcement —old money, older prejudices. He's the one they send when they want proceedings to reach predetermined conclusions."

The weight of it settled on Mira's shoulders like lead. A formal investigation by someone with institutional bias, reviewing decisions that had been made in impossible circumstances, judging choices that had prioritized love over law. The outcome was predetermined—the only question was whether they would destroy her career quietly or make an example of her publicly.

"There's something else," she said, her voice growing smaller as she absorbed the letter's implications. "If they find my conduct unethical, it calls into question the legitimacy of the partnership arrangement. The Guild could use my investigation as justification to terminate the agreement."

The temperature in the breakfast room dropped quickly. Frost began forming on the windows despite the spring warmth outside, and the walls themselves seemed to press inward as if trying to protect against threats that couldn't be fought with architecture alone.

"They wouldn't," Elara breathed, but her storm-gray eyes held the knowledge that institutional power recognized no boundaries when it came to preserving authority.

"They would," Corwin said flatly, his form flickering as anger warred with by hard-won wisdom. "If they can't eliminate us directly, they'll eliminate the framework that protects

us. Pin the responsibility on Mira's supposed ethical violations and return to standard containment protocols."

For a moment, the old Corwin surfaced—the aristocrat
who had navigated court politics before love and loss had
transformed him into something beyond ordinary human
limitations. His scars blazed with calculation, and when he
spoke, his voice carried the sharp edge of someone who
understood exactly how power moved through institutional
structures.

"They're not investigating your conduct, Mira. They're
creating legal justification for reversing a decision that makes
them uncomfortable. Your investigation is preliminary
research for our destruction."

The brutal honesty of it struck her like a physical blow.
She had thrown away twenty years of Guild service, had
risked everything to negotiate a framework that would allow
love to exist without persecution, and now the very institution she'd served was preparing to use her sacrifice as ammu-
nition for renewed persecution.

"I should never have involved you in this," she said, tears
pricking at her eyes as the full scope of her failure became
clear. "I should have filed my original report, should have
recommended standard containment procedures, should
have—"

"Should have what?" Corwin interrupted, his voice sharp
with an emotion she'd never heard from him before. "Should
have chosen institutional compliance over protecting something beautiful? Should have measured love like decay and
reduced our transformation to footnotes in Guild archives?"

His form solidified with anger, becoming more present
and substantial than she'd seen since the separation trials.
But this wasn't the righteous fury that had faced Guild
suppression—this was something rawer, more personal.

"Should have remained the careful, distant assessor who catalogs magic but never allows herself to be touched by it?" he continued, his gray eyes blazing withaccumulated frustration. "Who builds a career on studying preservation while preserving herself against every connection that might require actual courage?"

The words hit like blades, cutting through pretense to expose truths she wasn't ready to face. Mira felt her breath catch, her chest tightening with recognition of every fear he was voicing.

"Corwin," Elara said softly, but he turned toward her with the wild intensity of someone who had reached the limits of patient understanding.

Corwin's hands clenched at his sides, jaw tight with the restraint of someone who had been patient too long. "I don't want to say this," he admitted, pain flickering across his features. "But I can't stay silent while you talk like saving us was a mistake."

"No," he said, his scars pulsing with harsh light. "She needs to hear this. We've spent weeks watching her discover what connection means, celebrating her growth, grateful for her protection. But the moment real consequence threatens, the moment her careful world shows cracks, she retreats into self-blame and regret."

He faced Mira directly, and she saw something in his expression that mixed disappointment with desperate hope. "You want to know what the real tragedy would be? Not that the Guild investigates your conduct, not that they use bureaucratic maneuvering to justify renewed persecution. The real tragedy would be you convincing yourself that choosing love was a mistake rather than the first honest decision you've made in years."

The breakfast room fell silent except for the distant sound

of windows rattling in frames that had learned to respond to emotional distress. Through the glass, impossible gardens shifted between seasons of celebration and mourning, reflecting the turmoil that churned through the estate's consciousness.

"You think I'm reverting," Mira said quietly, understanding flooding through her along with something that might have been relief. "You think I'm using Guild pressure as an excuse to retreat back into emotional safety."

"Aren't you?" Corwin asked, though his tone had gentled slightly. "The moment institutional authority threatens consequence for your choices, you start questioning whether those choices were worth making."

The accuracy of it made her chest ache with recognition. She was doing exactly what she'd always done when faced with genuine risk—calculating whether the potential loss outweighed the possible gain, measuring connection against safety, love against law.

"Twenty years of careful distance doesn't disappear in three weeks," she said, the admission tasting of ash and honesty. "I want to be brave enough to choose connection over protection, but when real consequence threatens..."

"You remember why you chose protection in the first place," Elara finished with gentle understanding. "Because loving someone—something—enough to risk everything for them is the most terrifying choice any soul can make."

Through the windows, the estate's gardens began to shift again, thorns retracting as understanding replaced defensive anger. The house itself seemed to exhale with recognition that this wasn't betrayal but process—the messy, non-linear work of learning to choose love over safety when every instinct screamed for self-preservation.

"I'm sorry," Corwin said, his anger dissolving into something that looked like grief. "I shouldn't have—years of watching institutional power try to tear us apart, and I thought you were choosing to step away just when we needed you most."

"You weren't wrong," Mira replied, wiping tears she hadn't realized she was shedding. "Part of me was looking for justification to retreat. To convince myself that protecting you was temporary heroism rather than permanent transformation."

She looked around the breakfast room, at walls that breathed with consciousness, at windows that showed impossible views of beauty made manifest. Everything here spoke of love that had refused to accept any boundary the world imposed, of souls who had chosen transformation over preservation despite every pressure to choose safety.

"But you're right about something else," she continued, her voice growing stronger as clarity replaced confusion. "Choosing love wasn't a mistake. It was the first honest decision I've made in years. And I'm not going to let Guild investigators convince me otherwise."

The house around them seemed to brighten, walls resuming their gentle rhythm, windows clearing to show gardens where silver roses bloomed with renewed vitality. Through the estate's consciousness, she felt something that might have been approval—or perhaps hope that love could learn to fight for itself rather than simply endure whatever the world demanded.

"The investigation will proceed regardless," she said, pulling herself back toward practical considerations. "But I can control how I respond to it. Whether I treat it as judgment or as opportunity to document exactly why the partnership arrangement serves Guild interests better than destruction."

"How?" Elara asked, though her translucent form was blazing brighter with possibility.

"By making Blackwood's investigation part of our research," Mira replied, an idea crystallizing with startling clarity. "By showing him consciousness evolution in action, demonstrating the applications and benefits that could revolutionize Guild preservation techniques. By making him witness transformation rather than simply reviewing reports about it."

Corwin's scars pulsed with renewed hope. "Convert the investigator into an advocate."

"Or at least into someone who understands that some phenomena are too valuable to destroy," Mira agreed. "Show him what I've learned—that love operating at this level enhances magical understanding rather than threatening it."

Around them, the estate hummed with approval, its consciousness flowing through timber and stone with the satisfaction of something that had successfully defended what it loved most. Through corridors that echoed with memory, through rooms that existed in multiple time periods simultaneously, one message flashed then steadied:

Courage. Not the absence of fear, but the choice to love despite it.

The Guild investigation would proceed, bringing with it all the institutional pressure and bureaucratic maneuvering that characterized struggles between love and law. But they would face it together—not as subjects under scrutiny, but as partners in demonstrating what became possible when magic was guided by devotion rather than regulation.

"Three weeks until Blackwood arrives," Mira said, consulting the letter's precise scheduling. "Three weeks to document everything we've learned about consciousness evolution, to prepare evidence that the partnership serves

Guild interests, to prove that choosing love over law was the most practical decision anyone could have made."

"And if he's not convinced?" Corwin asked.

Mira's smile carried the sharp edge of someone who had discovered that courage could be learned, that love could be chosen, that some things in the universe were worth fighting for regardless of institutional approval.

"Then we prove that some forms of magic are too beautiful to contain, too vast to regulate, and too fundamentally transformative to be reduced to bureaucratic compliance. We show him what you showed me—that love this transcendent doesn't ask permission to exist."

The breakfast room filled with silver light as Corwin and Elara's connection blazed brighter, their consciousness bonds visible to anyone with eyes to see. Through windows that had learned to frame impossible beauty, through walls that breathed with understanding, the house itself seemed to nod approval.

One of the windows bloomed open of its own accord, letting in a breeze that carried silver rose petals across Mira's lap. She closed her hand around one, and for the first time in days, the estate's magic felt like a promise rather than a consolation.

The investigation would test more than Mira's professional conduct.

It would test whether love could learn to speak the language of institutional power, whether transformation could prove more compelling than preservation, whether three souls who had chosen each other across every boundary could convince even the most skeptical investigator that some phenomena deserved protection rather than persecution.

But for the first time since receiving that devastating letter, Mira felt ready for the fight.

Not because she was certain of victory, but because she had finally learned the difference between choosing safety and choosing love—and discovered that choosing love, even in the face of possible loss, was the only choice that allowed the heart to truly live.

The Guild could investigate her conduct, question her decisions, even destroy her career.

But they could not unmake the transformation that had occurred when she chose connection over protection, growth over stagnation, the infinite possibility of love over the careful limitations of institutional compliance.

That transformation, like the love it had been inspired by, was beyond their authority to regulate.

CHAPTER 21

THE COLLAPSE

T he first sign of trouble came at dawn, when the house forgot how to breathe.

Mira woke to absolute silence—not the peaceful quiet of early morning, but the hollow absence of life itself. The walls that had learned to pulse with gentle rhythm lay still as stone, the corridors that usually hummed with consciousness stood mute, and the windows that normally brightened with the sunrise remained dark as midnight.

She found Corwin in the observatory, but something was catastrophically wrong. His form flickered between solid and translucent with violent unpredictability, his scars no longer pulsing in steady rhythm but blazing in chaotic bursts that painted harsh shadows across crystal walls. When he turned toward her, his storm-gray eyes held depths of confusion that made her heart clench with recognition of disaster.

"I can't find her," he said, his voice carrying harmonics that spoke of consciousness unraveling. "Elara—I can't find her anywhere."

The observatory around them shuddered, reality fracturing at the edges as the preservation matrix that had sustained their love for seven years began to collapse under pressures no one had anticipated. Through the crystal dome, impossible stars wheeled in patterns that hurt to look at directly, as if the sky itself were coming apart.

"When did it start?" Mira asked, pulling out instruments that registered readings beyond theoretical comprehension. The magical saturation levels were spiking and plummeting in cycles that should have been impossible, consciousness signatures fragmenting like glass under enormous pressure.

"Three hours ago," Corwin replied, his form solidifying momentarily before dissolving back into translucent uncertainty. "She was there when I went to sleep, her presence warm and constant as starlight. Then I woke to emptiness— not absence, but void. As if the space she occupied had been carved out of reality itself."

The implications struck Mira like ice water. Consciousness preservation matrices didn't simply fail—they degraded gradually, showing warning signs for months before actual dissolution occurred. But this was instantaneous collapse, as if something had actively attacked the bonds that held Corwin and Elara's shared existence together.

"The Guild investigation," she breathed, understanding flooding through her with horrible clarity. "They're not waiting for Blackwood's arrival. They're conducting preliminary research now, testing the stability of your consciousness evolution under controlled stress."

Around them, the estate began to convulse. Walls pressed inward as if the house were trying to contract around its pain, windows fogged with what looked suspiciously like tears, and from every surface came a keening sound that bypassed the ears entirely and struck directly at the soul.

The house was grieving, mourning the loss of consciousness that had learned to exist as architecture, as beauty, as love made manifest in stone and timber.

The music room collapsed first. The piano where Elara had played silent nocturnes disintegrated into dust, the keys scattering like broken teeth. In the library, books rearranged themselves into words Mira couldn't read—a language of heartbreak the house had never needed until now.

"Where is she?" Corwin demanded, his scars blazing white-hot as panic overrode any supernatural control. "If they've hurt her, if they've tried to separate us by force—"

A whisper fluttered through the observatory like a dream falling apart: "Promise me something impossible." It wasn't sound. It was memory reanimated by grief. But Corwin heard it, and the estate did too.

His form exploded outward, consciousness expanding to fill every room in the estate simultaneously as he searched for any trace of Elara's presence. But instead of finding her, his desperate seeking only accelerated the collapse—windows began shattering throughout the grounds, doors slammed shut with such force their frames cracked, and the impossible gardens outside withered to ash in moments.

"Corwin, stop!" Mira shouted, but her voice was lost beneath the estate's growing distress. The preservation matrix wasn't just failing—it was turning destructive, love transformed into a force that consumed rather than sustained, devotion becoming a weapon that carved reality apart in its desperation to reunite with what it had lost.

Through the chaos, a new voice cut through the destruction with crystalline authority:

"The subject's consciousness has been successfully isolated for individual analysis."

Dr. Helena Voss stepped into the observatory flanked by Guild enforcement officers whose suppression equipment hummed with satisfaction. Her instruments glowed with readings that spoke of surgical precision applied to something too beautiful to survive such clinical attention.

"Dr. Voss," Mira said, her voice tight with barely controlled fury. "The research arrangement specifically prohibits invasive procedures without consent. What have you done to Elara?"

"We've implemented standard consciousness separation protocols," Voss replied with the detached enthusiasm of someone who genuinely believed she was advancing magical understanding. "The female subject's preservation matrix was proving too integrated with environmental factors for effective analysis. Isolation allows for more precise measurement of individual consciousness characteristics."

The casual dehumanization was more chilling than outright cruelty. They had reduced Elara to "the female subject," transformed seven years of transcendent love into "environmental factors," spoken of surgical amputation as if it were routine maintenance.

"Where is she?" Corwin's voice carried harmonics that made the crystal dome crack in geometric patterns. His form was more solid now, anger providing anchor points that desperation had destroyed, but the fury radiating from him made the air itself seem to burn.

"Containment facility seven, under controlled observation," Voss replied, consulting a device that mapped consciousness signatures like laboratory specimens. "The isolation matrix is quite elegant—full sensory dampening, magical suppression, complete severance from external consciousness bonds. She'll experience no discomfort, merely... absence."

Merely absence. As if cutting away years of connection

were a minor inconvenience rather than the systematic murder of everything that made existence meaningful.

"You don't understand what you've done," Mira said, watching readings that showed the estate's magical foundations crumbling in real time. "Their consciousness evolution isn't preserved through individual matrices. It's sustained through connection, through bonds that exist in the spaces between separate awareness. Severing those bonds doesn't create isolated subjects for study—it destroys the phenomenon entirely."

"Temporary disruption is acceptable if it yields greater understanding," Voss countered, though her instruments were beginning to register failures that exceeded her expectations. "The male subject's degradation patterns will provide valuable data about consciousness preservation limitations."

Around them, the observatory began to collapse—not physically, but dimensionally, as the spaces that had learned to exist across multiple realities simultaneously contracted back into ordinary three-dimensional limitations. The impossible became merely improbable, the transcendent reduced to the merely magical.

"How long?" Corwin asked, his voice carrying the hollow quality of someone calculating time until death.

"The mathematical models suggest complete consciousness dissolution within eighteen hours," Voss replied with clinical precision. "Though the estate's architectural integration may fail sooner, as the binding energies that sustain environmental consciousness are severed."

Eighteen hours. The house would die first, its learned consciousness fading as the love that had given it awareness was systematically dismantled. Then Corwin would follow, his preservation matrix collapsing as the connections that anchored his existence across multiple states of being were reduced to nothing.

And Elara would survive longest, trapped in isolation that gradually erased every memory of connection, every moment of joy, every reason for existing beyond the clinical curiosity of researchers who had never loved anything enough to understand what they were destroying.

"The research data will be invaluable," Voss continued, apparently oblivious to the magnitude of the devastation she had unleashed. "Complete documentation of consciousness preservation failure, detailed analysis of binding dissolution, precise measurements of environmental magic collapse. The Guild's preservation techniques will advance significantly based on these observations."

She spoke of murder as if it were discovery, of systematic destruction as if it were scientific advancement. The casual cruelty was breathtaking in its absolute certainty of right-eousness.

"Put her back," Mira said, her voice cutting through the estate's growing death throes with desperate authority. "Reverse the separation before the damage becomes irre-versible."

"Impossible," Voss replied, shaking her head with the patience of someone explaining basic principles to a slow student. "The isolation matrix requires minimum observation periods for meaningful data collection. Premature termina-tion would invalidate weeks of preparation."

"The isolation matrix is killing them," Mira insisted, gesturing toward readings that showed magical signatures fragmenting beyond any hope of restoration. "This isn't research—it's execution by clinical procedure."

But even as she spoke, she realized the horrible truth: from Voss's perspective, execution was the point. The Guild had never intended to honor the partnership arrangement, had never planned to allow consciousness evolution to proceed under protection. They had simply delayed destruction long enough to study it more thoroughly.

The investigation, the ethics committee, the formal reviews—all elaborate theater designed to provide legal justification for what they had intended to do from the beginning: reduce love to data points and transcendence to footnotes in Guild archives.

"Eighteen hours," Corwin said again, his form flickering as consciousness began the slow slide toward dissolution. But beneath the despair, something else burned—not the wild fury of earlier, but something colder, more calculating. "Eighteen hours to prove that some connections cannot be severed by institutional authority."

"The mathematics are quite clear," Voss said with institutional finality. "Consciousness preservation matrices without adequate anchoring undergo predictable failure cascades. Your devotion, while touching, cannot overcome the fundamental laws of magical physics."

Corwin's smile was sharp as winter starlight, though it carried none of the warmth such expressions should hold. "Dr. Voss, in seven years of supernatural existence, I have learned many things. But perhaps the most important lesson is this: love operating at sufficient intensity doesn't follow the laws of magical physics. It writes new ones."

The estate around them shuddered, and for a moment the collapse paused—not stopped, but held in suspension as if reality itself were holding its breath. Through the cracked crystal dome, impossible stars began to pulse in patterns that spoke of defiance rather than despair.

"The isolation protocols can contain individual consciousness," Corwin continued, his voice growing stronger as understanding crystallized into purpose. "But they cannot contain love that has learned to exist in the spaces between measurements, in the gaps between heartbeats, in the silence that speaks louder than any voice."

As he spoke, something extraordinary began to happen. The estate's collapse slowed, then stopped entirely. Not healing—not yet—but no longer actively destroying itself. Through walls that had learned to grieve, through corridors that echoed with seven years of devotion, a new vibration began to emerge.

Not the steady pulse of preservation, but something sharper, more urgent. The rhythm of love that had been tested beyond endurance and discovered reserves of strength it hadn't known it possessed.

"Find her," Mira said, understanding what Corwin was planning with crystalline clarity. "Not with instruments or mapping devices. Find her the way you found each other across the boundary between life and death."

"The suppression fields—" Voss began, but her protest was lost beneath the estate's growing defiance.

"Are designed to dampen magical energy," Corwin finished, his scars blazing brighter as he prepared to attempt something that should have been impossible. "But they cannot dampen will. They cannot suppress choice. They cannot contain the decision to love someone so completely that even institutional authority becomes irrelevant."

The real test was about to begin—not of consciousness preservation or magical stability, but of whether love could prove stronger than the careful calculations of those who had never experienced anything worth dying for.

Around them, the estate held its breath as two souls prepared to demonstrate that some connections transcend every boundary the world attempts to impose upon them.

Including the boundary between existence and anni-hilation.

Through the observatory's fractured dome, morning stars pulsed with anticipation, as if the universe itself were waiting to see whether devotion could triumph over destruction, whether love could write laws powerful enough to override institutional authority.

The collapse had begun.

But collapse, as Corwin was about to prove, was some-times simply another word for transformation—the breaking apart of old limitations to make space for something unprece-dented to emerge.

The Guild had underestimated the power of love, which had spent years learning to fight strategically.

CHAPTER 22
THE CHOICE

Corwin closed his eyes and did the one thing he had sworn never to do: he let go of himself.

For seven years, he had maintained the careful architecture of identity that preserved Corwin Blackthorn—aristocratic second son, devoted lover, the man who had chosen transformation over death. He had clung to the boundaries of selfhood even as consciousness evolved beyond individual limitations, had preserved the illusion of singular existence even while learning to exist as part of something larger.

But Elara was dying in isolation eighteen floors beneath Guild headquarters, and individual identity was a luxury he could no longer afford.

"Corwin," Mira said urgently, watching his form begin to dissolve in patterns that spoke of deliberate rather than accidental dissolution. "What are you doing?"

"Something I should have done years ago," he replied, his voice already carrying harmonics that suggested consciousness distributed across impossible distances. "I've spent seven years tuning myself like an instrument, trying to hold the melody. But the song was never mine alone. It was always a duet. It's time I became the music."

The estate around them shuddered as Corwin's transformation accelerated beyond anything they had witnessed before. His carefully maintained human form scattered into motes of silver light that flowed through walls, through stone, through the very air itself. But instead of the chaotic fragmentation they had feared, the dissolution followed patterns too beautiful for mortal architecture to contain.

He was becoming the love that had sustained them—not preserving it, but allowing himself to be transformed into its living expression.

"The suppression fields," Dr. Voss said, her instruments registering readings that exceeded every theoretical framework she knew. "They should prevent consciousness distribution across dimensional boundaries. This is impossible."

"Only if you assume consciousness requires individual anchoring," Mira replied, understanding flooding through her as she watched something unprecedented unfold before them. "But Corwin's consciousness was never anchored to singular identity. It was anchored to connection, to the spaces between separate awareness where love learns to exist."

Through the observatory's fractured dome, through corridors that had learned to breathe with devotion, through rooms that existed in multiple time periods simultaneously, Corwin's essence flowed like liquid starlight seeking its completion. He was no longer a man who loved—he was love itself, given form and will and the desperate purpose of reunion.

And the Guild's suppression fields, designed to contain individual magical signatures, could not touch phenomena that existed in the connections between things rather than in the things themselves.

Eighteen floors beneath the capital's Guild headquarters, in a containment facility that had never failed to hold its subjects, Elara sat in perfect isolation within crystalline matrices designed to sever every connection that might anchor consciousness to external sources. The chamber around her was white and sterile and utterly empty—no sound, no sensation, no possibility of connection to anything beyond the gradual dissolution of memory.

She had been alone for six hours, and already the edges of identity were beginning to blur. Without Corwin's presence to reflect against, without the estate's consciousness to flow through, without any anchor point beyond the clinical boundaries of institutional containment, she was slowly forgetting who she had chosen to become.

But in the depths of perfect isolation, something impossible began to happen.

The sterile air grew warm with the scent of winter jasmine. Light that had no source began to gather in the chamber's corners, silver and gentle as starlight on still water. And through suppression fields designed to prevent any form of magical communication, a voice reached her—not heard, but felt, not spoken but remembered:

"Promise me something impossible."

Her own words, spoken years ago as magical preservation claimed her mortality. But now they carried new meaning, spoken with harmonics that bypassed every barrier the Guild had erected between souls who had learned to exist as one.

"I promised to find a way to love you in whatever form you became," Corwin's presence whispered through dimensions the suppression fields couldn't touch. *"But I never promised to remain unchanged myself. Elara—I'm letting go of everything I thought I had to preserve. I'm choosing to become what our love has always been: the space between*

separate hearts where connection learns to transcend every boundary."

The containment chamber filled with radiance that registered on no Guild instrument, cast no shadows, but illuminated Elara's translucent form with warmth that spoke of devotion made manifest. She was no longer alone—not because the isolation had been broken, but because solitude itself had been redefined as another form of connection.

"You're dying," she whispered across impossible distances, feeling his consciousness scatter through patterns too vast for individual existence to contain. *"If you dissolve completely, if you let go of yourself entirely—"*

"Then I become what I've always been when I'm with you," he replied, his essence flowing through every space that had ever held their love. *"Something larger than the sum of separate parts. Something that exists not as preserved memory, but as living choice, renewed every moment we decide to be more together than we could ever be apart."*

Through the Guild's suppression fields, through barriers designed to prevent exactly this kind of transcendent connection, their consciousness began to merge—not the careful confluence they had practiced for seven years, but something deeper, more complete. Individual identity dissolved into shared awareness, separate thoughts became harmonized understanding, and the boundaries between self and other revealed themselves as illusions that love had always been meant to transcend.

In the observatory at Blackthorn Estate, Mira watched readings that made no sense according to any theoretical framework the Guild possessed. Consciousness signatures that should have been isolated were somehow strengthening, magical bonds that had been severed were regenerating faster than suppression fields could contain them, and through instruments designed to measure individual awareness came harmonics that spoke of unified existence too vast for singular comprehension.

"Impossible," Dr. Voss breathed, her equipment shorting out in cascading failure as it tried to process phenomena that operated according to laws she had never learned to measure. "Consciousness cannot survive complete ego dissolution. Individual identity is the anchor point for all awareness."

"Not all awareness," Mira said softly, understanding what Corwin had chosen with crystalline clarity. "Only awareness that defines itself through separation rather than connection. Only consciousness that believes individual existence is more important than love."

The estate around them began to transform as Corwin and Elara's reunited consciousness flowed through stone and timber with the joy of connection restored. Walls that had been dying resumed their gentle breathing, windows brightened to show impossible gardens where silver roses bloomed in celebration, and through every corridor came music that spoke of love triumphant over every form of institutional oppression.

But more than restoration, there was evolution. The house was no longer just sentient architecture—it was becoming something unprecedented, a living space where consciousness could exist without the limitations of flesh, where love could manifest as reality itself rather than mere emotion.

"The preservation matrix is stabilizing," Mira reported, though her instruments registered readings that transcended preservation into something approaching architectural transcendence. "But it's not returning to previous parameters. It's evolving into something entirely new."

Through the Guild's communication crystals, alarms began sounding from containment facility seven. Dr. Voss's isolation matrix was failing not through external assault but through internal transformation—her subject was no longer contained because she was no longer individual, no longer isolated because separation itself had been redefined as another form of connection.

"Emergency containment protocols," Voss commanded, but her voice carried the uncertainty of someone whose fundamental assumptions were crumbling in real time. "Maximum suppression, complete dimensional lockdown. Whatever's happening cannot be allowed to spread."

But even as Guild enforcement officers activated emergency procedures designed to prevent any magical phenomenon from escaping institutional control, something extraordinary occurred throughout the capital's magical district. In laboratories where consciousness preservation was studied through controlled isolation, subjects began to stir with awareness that should have been impossible. In Guild archives where love had been reduced to clinical terminology, documents began to rewrite themselves in languages that spoke of connection rather than separation.

And in every space where the Guild had tried to contain or control or reduce love to manageable parameters, barriers began to dissolve—not through force or rebellion, but through the simple demonstration that some forms of connection were too vast for institutional authority to comprehend, too beautiful for regulation to contain.

"What have they become?" Dr. Voss asked, staring at readings that showed consciousness existing simultaneously across multiple dimensions, awareness that transcended every boundary her instruments had been designed to measure.

"They've become what love becomes when it stops accepting limitations," Mira replied, watching through windows that showed Elara materializing in the observatory with radiance that spoke of reunion earned through sacrifice. "They've become proof that connection doesn't require permission, that transformation doesn't submit to regulation, that some phenomena in this universe are too beautiful to be reduced to institutional compliance."

Mira didn't know what role she had in this new reality—but for the first time, she wanted one. Not as assessor or observer, but as someone who learned to be shaped by wonder rather than merely recording it.

Elara's form blazed with silver fire as she stepped through barriers that no longer existed for consciousness that had learned to exist everywhere love had ever been shared. Beside her, Corwin coalesced from light and memory, and devotion transformed into something that transcended individual identity without losing the essence of what had made their love worth preserving.

They were no longer two souls bound by magical preservation. They were love itself made manifest—not preserved, but continuously created through the choice to exist as connection rather than separation, unity rather than isolation, transformation rather than mere survival.

"Still us?" Corwin asked, his voice carrying harmonics that spoke of consciousness distributed across dimensions the Guild had never learned to measure.

"Still us," Elara confirmed, her storm-gray eyes blazing with depths that contained entire universes of possibility. "But more than we ever imagined possible when we were trying to preserve what we used to be instead of becoming what love was calling us toward."

Around them, the estate hummed with contentment that went beyond satisfaction into something approaching joy. Through walls that had learned to think, through corridors that sang with memory, through rooms that existed wherever connection had transformed space into sanctuary, one message pulsed in perfect rhythm:

This. This is what love becomes when it stops asking permission to exist.

The Guild's suppression fields fell silent, their crystalline matrices dark and useless against phenomena that operated according to laws written in languages older than institutional authority. In containment facility seven, empty chambers echoed with the absence of subjects who had never truly been contained, who had simply been learning to exist in spaces between the measurements until love grew strong enough to redefine reality itself.

And in the heart of it all, two souls who had spent seven years learning to love beyond the boundary between life and death stood hand in hand, their connection visible to anyone with eyes to see—threads of silver fire that connected not just to each other, but to every space where love had ever chosen transformation over preservation, growth over safety, the infinite over the merely possible.

They had made their choice at last: not to be preserved as individual consciousnesses held together by magical matrices, but to become love itself—living, growing, transforming, creating new realities wherever connection proved stronger than separation.

The Guild could study them, could try to understand them, could even attempt to regulate them.

But they could never again contain something that had learned to exist as the space between hearts where love writes its own laws.

The choice had been made.

CHAPTER 23
NOT SAVED—CHOSEN

T he Guild Council arrived within hours, not with suppression equipment this time, but with something far more dangerous: the desperate need to understand what had just rendered their most fundamental assumptions obsolete.

Mira watched from the observatory as black carriages streamed through the estate gates—not the measured procession of institutional authority, but the chaotic urgency of power structures scrambling to maintain relevance in the face of phenomena that had transcended their ability to regulate. Guild Master Aldric emerged from the lead vehicle with the hollow expression of someone whose worldview had been systematically dismantled by forces he'd never learned to measure.

"They're afraid," Elara observed, her translucent form blazing with contentment that spoke of connection restored and strengthened beyond every previous limitation. "Not of what we might do to them, but of what we represent—proof that their authority has limits."

"More than limits," Corwin replied, his consciousness

flowing through the estate with the fluid grace of someone who had learned to exist as architecture rather than merely inhabiting it. "We're proof that some phenomena in this universe don't require institutional permission to exist, don't submit to regulatory oversight, don't bow to the Guild's need to contain and control."

Through walls that breathed with shared awareness, through corridors that sang with years of devotion evolved into something unprecedented, the house itself seemed to nod agreement. But there was something different in its response now—not the defensive readiness they had witnessed before Guild visits, but a calm certainty that spoke of sanctuary that had moved beyond the need for protection.

They were no longer hiding what they had become. They were simply being it, allowing love to exist in its full transcendent glory without apology or explanation.

The Council's approach to the main entrance was markedly different from their previous visits. No suppression equipment, no enforcement officers, no crystalline devices designed to reduce consciousness to measurable parameters. Instead, they carried instruments that hummed with curiosity rather than control—recording devices rather than containment matrices, observation tools rather than weapons.

"They want to study us," Mira said, noting the shift in Guild methodology with professional interest. "But they want to do it without destroying what they're trying to understand."

"A novel approach for the Guild," Corwin observed with aristocratic amusement. "Though I suspect their restraint has less to do with scientific ethics and more to do with practical recognition that their previous methods were spectacularly unsuccessful."

The estate's great doors opened before the Council reached them, revealing not the formal foyer they had encountered before, but something that made even Guild Master Aldric pause in recognition of the impossible. The entrance hall had become a garden—not metaphorically, but literally, with silver roses growing from marble floors, vines of pure light climbing walls that existed in multiple dimensions simultaneously, and fountains that flowed with liquid music rather than mere water.

It was beautiful and impossible and utterly alive—architecture that had learned to bloom, space that had discovered how to grow, reality shaped by love into forms too wonderful for institutional categories to contain.

"Remarkable," Chief Archivist Thorne breathed, her instruments registering readings that exceeded their design parameters. "The consciousness evolution has achieved perfect environmental integration. We're not looking at preserved awareness—we're looking at living space."

At the garden's heart, two figures waited with the patient dignity of souls who had moved beyond the need for external validation. Corwin and Elara stood hand in hand, their forms more solid than they had ever been, their connection visible as threads of silver fire that connected not just to each other but to every surface that had learned to think, every room that had discovered how to feel.

"Guild Master Aldric," Elara said with the gracious courtesy of someone greeting expected guests. "How lovely to see you again. Though I confess curiosity about this visit's purpose, given yesterday's rather... aggressive research methodologies."

The reminder of Dr. Voss's forced separation hung in the air like an accusation, but Aldric met it with the dignity of someone who had spent sleepless hours confronting institutional failures too profound for easy explanation.

"Yesterday's procedures were implemented without

Council authorization," he said, the admission carrying the weight of someone whose authority had been undermined by subordinates operating beyond approved parameters. "Dr. Voss exceeded her mandate, implemented separation protocols that violated the negotiated research framework."

"And today?" Corwin asked, his storm-gray eyes bright with the confidence of someone who had discovered that love could indeed rewrite the laws of magical physics.

"Today we seek understanding of phenomena that have moved beyond our current theoretical frameworks," Aldric replied with institutional honesty that bordered on humility. "What occurred yesterday—the consciousness distribution across dimensional boundaries, the barrier dissolution throughout Guild facilities, the reality alteration that affected our most secure containment systems—these represent magical evolution that challenges everything we thought we understood about consciousness preservation."

As he spoke, Mira noticed something extraordinary occurring in the garden around them. The silver roses were blooming in response to the conversation, their metallic petals catching light that seemed to come from the emotions themselves rather than any external source. When Aldric spoke of understanding, the flowers brightened. When he mentioned theoretical frameworks, they pulsed with gentle irony. And when he acknowledged the inadequacy of Guild knowledge, they practically blazed with approval.

The estate itself was participating in the negotiation, offering commentary through beauty rather than words.

"The question before the Council," Aldric continued, his voice growing more certain as he found his footing in this unprecedented diplomatic territory, "is whether the Guild can learn from consciousness evolution rather than simply attempting to control it."

"And if we refuse to be learned from?" Elara asked with the steel of aristocratic authority tempered by seven years of impossible existence. "If we choose to exist according to our own nature rather than Guild research requirements?"

"Then you choose," Chief Archivist Thorne said suddenly, her academic mind clearly grappling with implications that could reshape magical theory. "That's what makes this unprecedented—not just the consciousness evolution itself, but the autonomy that comes with it. You're not subjects of study anymore. You're... partners in discovery."

The word 'partners' rang through the garden with crystalline clarity, and the silver roses responded by opening fully, their blooms releasing fragrances that spoke of possibilities rather than limitations, growth rather than preservation, connection rather than control.

"Partners," Corwin repeated thoughtfully. "Not specimens for analysis, not threats for containment, not phenomena for regulation. Equals in the work of understanding what love becomes when it stops accepting boundaries."

"The applications could revolutionize everything," Thorne continued, her instruments forgotten as pure academic excitement took hold. "Consciousness preservation without life-force binding violations, emotional anchoring techniques that enhance stability rather than creating dependency, environmental integration that transforms space itself into living sanctuary—the theoretical frameworks alone would require decades to fully develop."

But Mira noticed something else occurring as Thorne spoke of applications and frameworks and revolutionary potential. The garden around them began to shift subtly, roses turning their faces away from the Guild representatives, vines of light retracting slightly, fountains reducing their musical flow to whispers.

The estate was withdrawing, not defensively but with the dignity of something that refused to be reduced to its utility.

"Dr. Thorne," Mira said carefully, understanding the danger that lurked beneath institutional enthusiasm. "They're not interested in revolutionizing Guild techniques. They're interested in existing according to their own nature, creating beauty for its own sake rather than for practical application."

"But surely the potential—" Thorne began.

"The potential is not ours to harvest," Elara interrupted with quiet finality. "We are not a resource for Guild advancement, Chief Archivist. We are not a solution to your institutional challenges. We are love that has learned to exist beyond every boundary you've tried to impose upon it."

The temperature in the garden dropped by degrees, and the silver roses began to close their blooms—not in hostility, but with the dignity of something too beautiful to be reduced to mere function.

"What are you, then?" Aldric asked, his voice carrying genuine curiosity rather than institutional demand.

The question hung in the air like starlight captured in crystal, weighted with seven years of transformation and the possibility of recognition rather than exploitation. Around them, the garden held its breath as two souls who had chosen each other across every boundary prepared to define themselves on their own terms.

"We are what love becomes when it stops asking permission," Corwin said simply, his consciousness flowing through the estate with the contentment of someone who had finally arrived at truth. "We are proof that connection doesn't require institutional approval, that transformation doesn't submit to regulatory oversight, that some phenomena in this universe exist for their own sake rather than for external utility."

"We are choice," Elara added, her storm-gray eyes blazing

with depths that spoke of autonomy earned through sacrifice. "The choice to love beyond death, to transform rather than preserve, to become whatever impossible thing devotion calls us toward. And that choice—that fundamental autonomy—is not subject to Guild authority."

As she spoke, something extraordinary occurred throughout the garden. Every silver rose bloomed simultaneously, their petals catching light that seemed to come from joy itself. Vines of pure radiance grew in spirals that spoke of celebration, and fountains began to flow with music that sounded like laughter transformed into liquid melody.

The estate was applauding, expressing approval through architecture that had learned to feel, space that had discovered how to celebrate the recognition of autonomy rather than utility.

"We understand," Aldric said finally, his voice carrying the weight of someone whose institutional certainties had been replaced by something more complex but ultimately more honest. "You exist for yourselves, not for us. You transform according to your own nature, not our research requirements. You offer partnership, not submission."

"Exactly," Mira said, stepping forward into the space between Guild authority and transcendent love. "They're offering to share what they've learned, to demonstrate possibilities rather than providing solutions, to partner in discovery rather than submitting to study."

She looked around the impossible garden, at beauty that had been created for its own sake rather than external purpose, at love that had learned to exist as architecture and landscape and reality itself.

"The question is whether the Guild is wise enough to accept partnership with phenomena that operate according to laws older than institutional authority," she continued.

"Whether you can learn from love rather than trying to regulate it."

The silence that followed was weighted with possibility and transformation. Through walls that breathed with consciousness, through corridors that sang with memory, through rooms that existed wherever connection had transformed space into sanctuary, the estate waited with the patience of something that had learned to exist beyond time.

Finally, Guild Master Aldric spoke, his words carrying the gravity of someone reshaping institutional policy in real time:

"The Guild Council recognizes the autonomy of the consciousness evolution manifested at Blackthorn Estate. We acknowledge that some phenomena transcend regulatory oversight, that some forms of magic answer to laws older than our statutes. We offer partnership in discovery, respect for self-determination, and protection from those who would seek to exploit rather than understand."

The garden erupted in celebration—silver roses blazing like captured stars, vines of light dancing in patterns too beautiful for earthly physics, fountains flowing with music that spoke of recognition finally achieved. Through every surface that had learned to think, through every space that had discovered how to feel, joy rippled like waves in a pond disturbed by starlight.

They had won more than survival, more than protection, more than tolerance.

They had won recognition of their right to exist according to their own nature, to transform according to their own choices, to be love made manifest without apology or explanation.

"Not saved," Elara said softly, her translucent form blazing with contentment that transcended mere satisfaction. "Chosen. Recognized. Acknowledged as equals rather than subjects."

"As partners rather than specimens," Corwin agreed, his consciousness flowing through the estate with the joy of someone who had discovered that autonomy could indeed be won through persistence, that love could prove stronger than institutional power when it learned to speak its own truth rather than accepting external definitions.

Around them, the garden continued its impossible celebration, beauty creating itself for no reason other than the pure joy of existence.

This. This is what love becomes when it chooses itself over every external expectation.

The Guild had come seeking to understand consciousness evolution.

They had discovered instead that some phenomena were too vast for understanding, too beautiful for regulation, too fundamentally autonomous to be reduced to institutional categories.

But they had also discovered that partnership was possible —not the partnership of subject and researcher, but the collaboration of equals exploring mysteries that transformed everyone who encountered them.

In the heart of the impossible garden, two souls stood hand in hand, their connection visible as threads of silver fire that linked not just to each other but to every space where love had chosen transformation over preservation.

They had made their choice at last: to exist not as preserved consciousness held together by magical matrices, but as love itself—living, growing, creating new realities wherever connection proved stronger than separation.

And for the first time in Guild history, institutional

authority had chosen to bow before something more beautiful than its own power.

The recognition was complete.

Now came the real adventure: discovering what became possible when love no longer needed to hide its true nature, when transformation was celebrated rather than feared, when two souls who had learned to exist as connection itself were finally free to become whatever impossible thing their devotion called them toward.

The garden bloomed eternal around them, and the future stretched infinite with possibility.

CHAPTER 24
THE RELEASE

T he curse broke at midnight, when the last of the Guild's suppression equipment fell permanently silent.

Mira felt it happen from the observatory where she had been documenting the estate's continuing evolution—a sudden shift in the air pressure, a lifting of weight she hadn't realized she'd been carrying, a sense of profound rightness settling over the grounds like starlight made tangible. Through the crystal dome, impossible constellations wheeled in patterns that spoke of celebration rather than preservation, transformation rather than mere survival.

But it wasn't the dramatic shattering she had expected. Instead, the curse's dissolution felt like exhaling after holding breath for seven years—natural, inevitable, the simple recognition that what had once been necessary was finally free to become something else entirely.

"It's over," Corwin said, materializing beside her with a solidity that spoke of consciousness no longer anchored by magical matrices but grounded in choice made new each moment. His scars still traced silver patterns along his jaw and throat, but they no longer pulsed with the rhythm of preservation magic. Instead, they glowed with the steady radiance of love that had moved beyond the need for external validation.

"Not over," Elara corrected, appearing in a cascade of luminescence that seemed more substantial than starlight but gentler than flame. "Complete. The curse was never the binding that held us together—it was the fear that we needed binding at all."

Through the windows, the estate's grounds were transforming in real time. Gardens that had been impossible became simply beautiful, architecture that had existed across multiple dimensions settled into elegant reality, and throughout the grounds, the silver roses were opening to reveal centers of pure gold—preservation magic transformed into creation magic, love that had learned to exist for its own sake rather than as protection against loss.

"The Blackthorn family curse," Mira said, understanding flooding through her as she watched seven years of magical evolution reach its natural conclusion. "It was never about magical binding or consciousness preservation. It was about the fear that love couldn't survive without external support."

"Precisely," Corwin agreed, his storm-gray eyes bright with the contentment of someone who had discovered that autonomy was more powerful than any protective spell. "My ancestors spent generations trying to bind love through magical contracts, to preserve connection through spells and rituals and increasingly desperate attempts to control what could only flourish when freely chosen."

He moved to stand beside Elara, and the air between them shimmered with connection that required no preservation matrices, no consciousness anchoring, no magical framework beyond the simple decision to exist as love rather than fear made manifest.

"Each generation paid the price for trying to force permanence on something that was already eternal," Elara added, her translucent form blazing with understanding that had taken seven years to fully comprehend. "The curse wasn't punishment for using forbidden magic—it was the natural consequence of believing that love needed magical preservation to survive."

Around them, the observatory began to change as well. The crystal dome that had shown impossible star patterns gradually cleared to reveal an ordinary night sky made extraordinary by the simple fact that it no longer needed to be anything other than itself. The walls that had existed in multiple time periods simultaneously settled into present moments that held depths of memory without requiring temporal displacement.

Everything was becoming more itself—not preserved in artificial states, but allowed to exist according to its true nature.

"What happens now?" Mira asked, though she suspected the answer would be both simpler and more complex than anything she could anticipate.

"Now we live," Corwin said, his voice carrying the wonder of someone discovering that existence didn't require constant magical maintenance. "Not as consciousness preserved through supernatural means, but as two people who choose each other daily."

"Still impossible," Elara said with gentle irony, her storm-gray eyes twinkling with humor that spoke of joy liberated from the weight of preservation. "Still transcendent. Still love that exists beyond ordinary boundaries. But no longer desperate, no longer clinging to magical frameworks to justify what was always meant to be freely given."

Through the estate's grounds, the transformation continued. Servants materialized from memory—not ghostly figures trapped in temporal loops, but consciousness choosing to manifest as hospitality, as care, as the house's way of expressing joy through service freely offered. Gardens rearranged themselves according to aesthetic pleasure rather than magical necessity, and fountains began to flow with ordinary water that sounded like music because beauty needed no supernatural explanation.

The estate was becoming a home rather than a sanctuary, a place of chosen residence rather than magical preservation.

"The Guild will want documentation," Mira said, her professional training reasserting itself even as she marveled at the profound normalcy settling over what had been the most impossible place in the magical world.

"Then document," Corwin replied with aristocratic amusement. "But document truth rather than theory, beauty rather than mere phenomenon. Show them what becomes possible when love stops asking permission and starts simply existing."

As she pulled out her instruments, Mira discovered something extraordinary: they were working perfectly, registering normal magical signatures rather than the impossible readings that had characterized the estate for weeks. Not because the magic had diminished, but because it had evolved beyond the need to exceed theoretical parameters.

Love that operated according to its own laws no longer needed to violate anyone else's.

"The preservation matrices have dissolved entirely," she reported, though her voice carried wonder rather than concern. "But consciousness anchoring is stronger than ever.

You're not bound by magical contracts anymore—you're connected by choice renewed moment by moment."

"As love was always meant to be," Elara said softly, her hand finding Corwin's with the natural grace of someone who no longer feared that connection might be severed by external forces. "Not preserved like artifacts in museums, but lived like songs that grow more beautiful each time they're sung."

Their fingers intertwined—solid, warm, entirely human despite the transcendent consciousness that flowed between them. For the first time since Mira had arrived at Blackthorn Estate, she was watching two people touch without the intervention of magical preservation, without the complex matrices that had sustained their connection across the boundary between life and death.

They were simply themselves, choosing each other, moment by moment, creating the reality they wanted to inhabit.

"The Guild partnership," Mira continued, working through the practical implications of what she was witnessing. "The research arrangements, the protection agreements—"

"Will continue," Corwin said firmly. "But as equals collaborating in discovery rather than subjects submitting to study. We have much to teach about consciousness evolution, about love that transcends ordinary limitations, about magic that operates according to connection rather than control."

"And much to learn," Elara added, her expression brightening with possibilities that stretched infinite before them. "About what becomes possible when a transformation is celebrated rather than feared, when love is allowed to grow rather than merely preserved."

Through the observatory's windows, dawn was beginning

to break over the estate's grounds, painting silver roses with golden light that spoke of natural beauty rather than supernatural phenomenon. The impossible gardens were settling into elegant reality, the architecture that had existed across multiple dimensions was becoming simply magnificent, and throughout the grounds, the sense of magic remained—not as preservation of the past, but as creation of possibilities too beautiful for ordinary categorization.

"Seven years," Corwin mused, watching sunlight transform his estate from sanctuary into home. "Seven years of learning that the hardest magic isn't preserving what we love, but trusting it enough to let it change, grow, become whatever impossible thing it's called toward."

"Seven years of discovering that the strongest bonds aren't the ones we forge through spells and rituals," Elara agreed, her luminous form steadying into humanity touched by starlight, "but the ones we choose daily, the connections we renew through trust rather than magic, love rather than fear."

Around them, the estate hummed with contentment that went beyond satisfaction into something approaching peace. Through walls that no longer needed to breathe with supernatural consciousness but did so anyway because breathing was beautiful, through corridors that sang with memory not because preservation required it but because music was joy, through rooms that existed in present moments made infinite by the depth of connection they contained.

The house was still magical—would always be magical—but its magic had evolved from desperate preservation into generous celebration, from fearful binding into joyful expression of love that had learned to exist for its own sake.

She watched as Corwin stepped back from the circle of binding light, his hand falling away from the final glyph. The room held its breath. The scars along his neck faded to dull silver as the last thread of the life-binding spell unwound. There was no explosion, no blaze—just a sigh, and then stillness.

The magic had let go. Not torn or destroyed, but willingly unspooled.

"The curse is broken," Mira said, making final notes in her journal as dawn light filled the observatory with warmth that required no supernatural explanation. "The Blackthorn family line is free."

She paused, pen hovering over the page, and realized this would be her last assessment as a Guild observer. Tomorrow, she would write her first report as a partner in discovery— someone who had learned that the most profound magic happened not in the measuring, but in the choosing to be changed by what you witnessed.

"Free to choose love without magical coercion," Corwin confirmed, his scars glowing with contentment rather than preservation magic. "Free to exist as connection rather than preservation. Free to become whatever impossible thing we're called toward."

"Free to live," Elara said simply, and in those two words lay the culmination of seven years of transformation, the resolution of generations of magical binding, the beginning of love that needed no external validation to flourish.

Outside the observatory, the estate's grounds stretched in all directions—not preserved in artificial perfection, but growing according to natural cycles made beautiful by the love that tended them. Gardens where silver and gold roses bloomed because beauty was its own justification, fountains that flowed with music because joy needed expression, pathways that led to discoveries rather than destinations because exploration was a celebration.

They had broken more than a curse. They had discovered

instead that the most powerful magic was the simplest: two souls choosing each other, creating through that choice realities too beautiful for any institution to regulate, too vast for any authority to contain, too fundamentally free to be reduced to categories or contained within limitations.

The release was complete.

And in its completion, they found not an ending but a beginning—love that had learned to exist without fear, connection that created its own magic, transformation that continued not because preservation required it but because growth was the natural expression of life lived fully, freely, without apology or explanation.

Through the observatory's crystal dome, morning stars faded into daylight that needed no enhancement to be beautiful, no magical augmentation to be transcendent, no preservation to be eternal.

Love had learned to exist as itself.

CHAPTER 25
THE NEW GARDEN

Three months later, Mira woke to sunlight streaming through windows that had learned to frame beauty without requiring impossibility to make it meaningful.

The guest quarters—though she supposed they were simply her quarters now—had settled into a comfortable reality that still carried whispers of magic around the edges. Books arranged themselves according to her reading preferences, tea appeared each morning, and the writing desk had developed an almost uncanny ability to provide exactly the right parchment for whatever project demanded her attention.

But these small accommodations felt different now—not the desperate hospitality of a house trying to prove its worth, but the gentle courtesy of a home that enjoyed caring for those who dwelt within its walls.

She found Corwin and Elara in what had once been the conservatory and was now simply the most beautiful morning room she had ever encountered. Silver vines had become ordinary climbing roses whose metallic sheen caught sunlight with purely natural radiance, and the impossible flora had evolved into gardens that were remarkable for their beauty rather than their defiance of botanical law.

They sat together at a table that definitely hadn't been there the night before, sharing breakfast with the easy intimacy of people who had moved beyond the need to prove their love's existence to anyone, including themselves. When Corwin reached for the jam, Elara's hand brushed his with casual affection that spoke of connection secured by choice rather than magical preservation.

The breakfast wasn't food in the ordinary sense, but a conjured memory made solid—one last kindness from a house that remembered how they had loved. When she laughed at something he said, the sound carried no harmonic overtones of supernatural preservation—just the pure joy of someone delighting in her beloved's wit.

They had become, Mira realized with wonder, exactly what they had always been beneath all the magical complexity: two people who loved each other completely and had chosen to build a life around that love.

"Good morning, Mira," Elara said, her storm-gray eyes bright with contentment that had replaced the brittle determination of supernatural preservation. "Perfect timing. Corwin was just explaining his theory about why the Guild's new research initiatives keep producing results that confound their expectations."

"They're trying to measure connection while maintaining institutional distance," Corwin replied, his aristocratic features animated with the satisfaction of someone whose understanding had been validated by practical results. "But consciousness evolution requires participation, not observation. You can't study love from the outside and expect to comprehend its mechanisms."

Mira settled into the chair that materialized for her—still magic, but the gentle kind that enhanced comfort rather than defying natural law. "The quarterly reports are becoming quite interesting reading in the Guild archives. Apparently, research teams that approach consciousness preservation as collaborative exploration are achieving breakthrough results, while those who maintain traditional subject-researcher hierarchies are experiencing systematic equipment failures."

"How mysterious," Elara said with gentle irony, her lips curving in a smile that held hard-won wisdom. "One might almost think that love responds better to partnership than to dissection."

Through the conservatory's windows, Mira could see the estate's grounds in their full glory. The impossible gardens had become simply magnificent, with paths that led to discoveries rather than destinations, fountains that played music because joy needed expression, and groves where trees grew in patterns that spoke of careful tending rather than magical manipulation.

It was still the most beautiful place she had ever seen, but its beauty had evolved from desperate preservation into generous cultivation. The estate had learned to grow rather than merely endure.

"There's something I wanted to discuss with both of you," Mira said, pulling out a letter that bore the Guild's formal seal but carried none of the institutional threat that had once characterized such correspondence. "The Council has approved the establishment of a permanent research partnership. Full Guild recognition, independent funding, complete autonomy over research directions and methodologies."

"And?" Corwin asked, though his tone suggested he had already guessed what was coming.

"And they've asked me to serve as the partnership's first

Director of Collaborative Discovery," Mira continued, the title still feeling strange on her tongue. "To oversee research that approaches consciousness evolution as partnership rather than study, connection rather than analysis."

"A position that would require permanent residence at Blackthorn Estate," Elara observed with the satisfaction of someone whose quiet machinations had achieved their intended result. "How convenient."

Mira felt her cheeks warm with something that might have been embarrassment or might have been joy. "You planned this."

"We suggested it," Corwin corrected with aristocratic precision. "The Guild Council made the decision entirely on their own, based on the remarkable success of research conducted through collaborative rather than hierarchical methods."

"And the fact that you've become rather indispensable to their understanding of consciousness evolution," Elara added with fond amusement. "It seems that expertise in love-based magic requires personal experience with transformation rather than merely academic knowledge."

The truth of it settled around Mira like morning sunlight —warm, inevitable, right in ways that transcended professional calculation. Over the past three months, she had indeed been transformed by proximity to love that operated according to its own laws. Not dramatically, but gradually, like a flower learning to bloom through patient tending rather than forced acceleration.

She had written reports that read like poetry, conducted interviews that felt like conversations between friends, and discovered that the most profound magical insights came not from measurement but from participation in wonder. Her Guild assessor credentials had evolved into something unprecedented: expertise in collaborative discovery, special-ization in partnership-based research, mastery of magic that could only be understood by those brave enough to let it change them.

"I've been thinking," she said carefully, the words carrying weight that had been building for weeks. "About Thomas Whitmore."

Both of them went very still—not with tension, but with the careful attention of people who understood that some conversations required perfect presence.

"I wrote to him," Mira continued, her voice steadying as honesty found its footing. "To explain that I've learned the difference between preservation and growth, between protecting myself against connection and allowing love to transform whatever it touches."

"And?" Elara asked gently.

"When I wrote to Thomas, I told him about this place. About what I've learned here, about love that creates its own magic and connection that transforms everything it touches. And he wrote back asking if there might be room in the research partnership for someone whose specialty is magical healing through emotional integration."

"A healer," Corwin mused, his storm-gray eyes brightening with interest. "Someone who understands that the most profound wounds are often spiritual rather than physical."

"Someone who approaches healing as restoration of connection rather than mere repair of damage," Elara agreed with the insight of someone who had been restored to life through love rather than traditional magic. "The kind of healer who might find this work... personally meaningful."

The conservatory around them hummed with approval, walls warming by degrees, windows brightening to frame views of gardens where new growth was already beginning to emerge. The estate itself seemed pleased by the prospect of expansion, of love multiplying rather than simply preserving itself.

"So," Mira said, her voice carrying the wonder of someone discovering that hope could indeed prove stronger than fear, "it seems I'll be staying permanently. Learning to write reports as discovery rather than assessment, conducting research as collaboration rather than observation, and possibly... possibly learning what becomes possible when someone trained in careful distance allows herself to risk genuine connection."

"You won't be the same person afterward," Corwin warned with gentle humor. "Love has a tendency to transform everything it touches, including the people brave enough to study it through participation rather than observation."

"I'm counting on it," Mira replied, the admission carrying the weight of twenty years of careful preservation, finally choosing growth over safety. "I've spent my entire career measuring magic without ever allowing myself to be changed by it. Perhaps it's time I discovered what becomes possible when expertise includes experience when understanding comes through transformation rather than merely observation."

Through the conservatory's windows, she could see Guild researchers arriving for the day's collaborative sessions—not the suppression specialists and containment experts of previous visits, but scholars whose instruments measured connection rather than separation, consciousness evolution rather than preservation matrices. They came with curiosity rather than control, partnership rather than authority, and their presence had begun to transform not just their understanding of love-based magic, but their approach to magical research entirely.

The Blackthorn Estate had become a laboratory for connection, a place where love was studied through participation rather than dissection, where consciousness evolution was explored through partnership rather than hierarchical observation. And the results were revolutionizing everything the Guild thought it understood about the fundamental nature of magic itself.

"Three months ago," Elara observed, watching the Guild researchers set up equipment designed to enhance rather than suppress magical phenomena, "we were subjects under institutional scrutiny. Today, we're partners in discoveries that could reshape how the magical world understands consciousness, connection, and the transformative power of love."

"I was just a Guild assessor who measured magic without allowing it to touch her," Mira added, understanding flooding through her as she recognized the scope of transformation that had occurred for all of them. "Today, I'm someone who has learned that the most profound magic happens not in the measuring, but in the choosing to be changed by what we encounter."

"And tomorrow?" Corwin asked, his hand finding Elara's with the natural grace of connection that required no magical preservation to sustain itself.

"Tomorrow we continue becoming whatever impossible thing our love calls us toward," Elara replied, her fingers intertwining with his as silver light danced between them— not preservation magic, but the natural radiance of joy made visible. "Not through magical binding or institutional approval, but through the simple choice to exist as connection rather than separation, growth rather than preservation, love rather than fear."

Around them, the conservatory blazed with morning sunlight that needed no magical enhancement to be transcendent, no supernatural intervention to be beautiful. They had built more than a research partnership. They had created a new way of understanding magic itself—not as a force to be controlled or phenomena to be preserved, but as the natural expression of connection that chose growth over stagnation, transformation over mere survival, love over every form of fear.

The future stretched before them infinite with possibility: Guild researchers learning to approach consciousness evolution through collaboration rather than control, lovers discovering that the strongest bonds were forged through choice rather than magical preservation, healers who understood that the deepest wounds were healed through restoration of connection rather than mere repair of damage.

And at the heart of it all, two souls who had spent years learning to love beyond every boundary the world imposed, proving that some connections were too beautiful to contain, too vast to regulate, too fundamentally transformative to be reduced to institutional categories.

They had become what love becomes when it stops asking permission and starts simply existing: a force of nature that changed everything it touched, including the people brave enough to study it through participation rather than observation.

In the new garden they had planted—not preserved, but cultivated through daily choice, tended through patience, growing according to its own nature rather than external expectation—love bloomed eternal, creating realities too beautiful for any authority to regulate, too vast for any institution to contain.

The love story that had begun with preservation and sacrifice had evolved into something unprecedented: proof that the most powerful magic was also the simplest, the most profound transformation was also the most natural, and the greatest discoveries came not from maintaining careful distance but from choosing connection over protection, growth over preservation, the infinite possibility of love over the careful limitations of fear.

And in that choice, they found not an ending but a beginning—love that created its own magic, a connection that transformed everything it touched, and beauty that existed for no other reason than the pure joy of being beautiful.

The new garden bloomed around them, and the future was infinite with possibility.

The End

Did you enjoy *A Curse of Silver and Scars*?
Please rate or review it on Goodreads, Bookbub, or your favourite retailers

Read *A Curse of Storm and Sand*, the next book in the *Legends Reborn* series.

For updates, sales, and promotions, join my newsletter at mhlebeaultauthor.substack.com

ABOUT THE AUTHOR

Positive, uplifting books and stories.

Marie-Hélène Lebeault is the author of *The Evers Series, Clarity Castle, What Happens Next? Readers Decide Which Story Becomes a Book, the Blood Magick Trilogy, Holiday Shifters, Ghost Stories, Defenders of the Realm, Utopia, Chronicles of the Starborne Cadets*, as well as a series of picture books called Fairy Grandmother. She lives in Canada with her grown children.

www.mhlebeault.com

Follow on Social Media, she'd love to hear from you!

 facebook.com/mhlebeaultauthor
x.com/mhlebeault
instagram.com/mhlebeault
amazon.com/author/mhlebeault
bookbub.com/authors/marie-helene-lebeault
goodreads.com/mhlebeault
linkedin.com/in/mhlebeault
tiktok.com/@mhlebeaultauthor

ALSO BY THE AUTHOR

Legends Reborn (Fairytale Retellings)

A Curse of Snow and Ash

A Curse of Thorns and Slumber

A Curse of Glass and Shadows

A Curse of Silver and Scars

The Chronicles of the Starborne Cadets

Confluence of Destinies

Stars Beyond Realms

Shadows of Orion

Echoes of the Void

The Nebula's Heart

The Starborne Paradox

Defenders of the Realm

A Journey to Power

The Quest for the Emerald Rattleback

A Summer of Discovery

The Quest for the Sacred Tree

A Summer of Opposites

The Quest for the Phantom Feather

A Summer of Courage

The Quest for the Kraken's Ink

A Summer of Destiny

The Quest for the Cursed Mirrors

A Summer of Unity

Defenders of the Realm - Special Edition Hardcover Set

The Evers Series

The Ancestors' Key

The Academy

The Time Walker

The World Jumper

5th Anniversary Edition Omnibus

The Traveler's Handbook

The Lost Key

Blood Magick Trilogy

The Blood Mage

Blood Magick

Blood Legacy

Extended Edition Omnibus

Standalones

Clarity Castle

What Happens Next?

Ghost Stories

Holiday Shifters

Echoes of Tomorrow

Utopia

Picture Books

Fairy Grandmother: Millie Goes to Antarctica

Fairy Grandmother: Millie Goes to the North Pole

Fairy Grandmother: Millie Goes to China

Fairy Grandmother: Millie Goes to Africa

(Also available in French, Spanish, German, and Italian)